The Faber Book of Reflective Verse

also edited by Geoffrey Grigson

————

The Faber Book of Popular Verse
The Faber Book of Love Poems
The Faber Book of Epigrams and Epitaphs
The Faber Book of Nonsense Verse
The Faber Book of Poems and Places

The Faber Book of
REFLECTIVE VERSE

Edited by
Geoffrey Grigson

faber and faber
LONDON · BOSTON

First published in 1984
by Faber and Faber Limited
3 Queen Square London WC1N 3AU

Printed in Great Britain by
Redwood Burn, Trowbridge, Wiltshire
All rights reserved

This selection © Geoffrey Grigson, 1984

British Library Cataloguing in Publication Data

The Faber book of reflective verse.
1. Poetry—Translations into English
2. English poetry—Translations from foreign literature
I. Grigson, Geoffrey
808.81   PN6101

ISBN 0–571–13299–5
ISBN 0–571–13300–2 Pbk

To Sophie

Contents

[6]

[7]

[8]

[9]

[10]

Acknowledgements

For permission to reprint copyright material the editor and publishers gratefully acknowledge the following:

Curtis Brown Ltd for "A Vision" from *Selected Poems and Prose of John Clare*; and for "Hesperus" and "Song" ("Love Lives Beyond the Tomb") from *The Later Poems of John Clare 1837–1864* (OUP), © Eric Robinson 1984; reproduced by permission of Curtis Brown Ltd.

Faber and Faber Ltd for "A Summer Night", "Earth, Receive an Honoured Guest" (from "In Memory of W. B. Yeats") from *Collected Poems* and "Our News Is Seldom Good" from *New Year Letter*, all by W. H. Auden.

Faber and Faber Ltd for "Thalassa" from *The Collected Poems of Louis MacNeice*.

The Society of Authors as the literary representative of the Literary Trustees of Walter de la Mare and Faber and Faber Ltd for "The Comb", "A Robin", "The Old Summerhouse", "Winter Evening" from *The Complete Poems of Walter de la Mare*; the last three poems also appear in *The Collected Poems of Walter de la Mare*.

The Society of Authors as the literary representative of the Estate of A. E. Housman and Jonathan Cape Ltd for "Crossing Alone the Lighted Ferry" by A. E. Housman.

The society of Authors as the literary representative of the Estate of James Joyce for "O Sweetheart, Hear Thou" from "Poem XVIII" from *Chamber Music* by James Joyce.

Michael Yeats, Macmillan London Ltd and A. P. Watt Ltd for "The Wild Swans at Coole", "The Magi", "Under Bare Ben Bulben's Head" by W. B. Yeats.

Introduction

I hope that not too many readers of this collection—probably the last anthology I shall compile—are going to complain that it includes more familiar poems than they expect; even, they may think, more hackneyed poems. Such inclusions—along with a few others—are deliberate, collecting poems which are commonly felt to be, as most of us might say, "poetical" in the sense of being solemn, peaceful, musical and correspondent to the solemn and peaceful mood rather than the excited or ecstatic mood in ourselves, in our lives. There is another possible complaint that solemn and peaceful poems should be, or must always be, great poetry and that I have chosen—as I meant to—many poems for which the word "great" is not justified.

Take Leigh Hunt's "Abou Ben Adhem", for example. Why do we all know it? Why do we all (I think) enjoy it, and why are we able to repeat most of it without having deliberately learnt its stanzas by heart? We have said it over and over again to ourselves from childhood, perhaps not noticing that in a Christian sense it is not particularly a religious poem. But then we hope that like Abou Ben Adhem we love—on the whole—our fellow men. So here is a degree of the sententious we allow ourselves: here is an angel more on the side of our fellow men than on the express side of the particular god whom most of us may be thought to have loved and acknowledged (and to have dreaded) once upon a time. We may think this familiar god of ours has had plenty of lovers, and so can now do without those particular rhythms and expressions of religious love; which is one reason why on the whole I have excluded the customary poems of Christian belief which do not any longer serve for all of our at once tragic and happy race.

The publishers and I had some differences and discussions about the title. First of all I wanted to call this anthology *The Faber Book of Solemn Verse*. But how many readers would have thought of "solemn" as a special, indeed an attractive enough category, when there are all the other categories, comic poems, nonsense poems, satirical poems, light poems, let alone the specifically religious Christian verse? So I changed my mind. I became certainly against tying solemnity to a single set or cult or kind of belief and rationed myself to rather few poems of emphatic Christianity, inclining to leave out poems which look to reward for being good or kind, etc., in a future life.

All the same a kind of serenity or joyful solemnity which we can all accept, up to a point, is given us by that blessed and blessing poet, George Herbert, who recovers from illness and can so "relish versing", and whom I for one cannot omit.

One of my publishers threw at my head—and I welcomed it—something said by that doubting, worried, in some ways sceptical, not yet altogether despondent poet and thinker, Matthew Arnold, that "the grand style arises in poetry, when a noble nature, poetically gifted, treats with simplicity or with severity a serious subject." Yet greatness and grandeur do not exhaust the desirable pleasures of the fairly solemn and peaceable, and simple.

Some poems in this collection—a few poems—may be thought, if solemn, decidedly unpeaceful, even violent or redolent of violence. But a statement of violence or despair or defeat may in its rhythms be conducive of just the human attitudes, the human comfort, which I have also had in mind and which help to justify and explain calling this anthology one of reflective verse—verse that induces reflection.

I admit to one other consideration. Poetically we have been living through a very odd time, in part through the morbid investigation of psychology, in part through a determination to renew and so reject much—and this must include many poems we used to respect and love—in the ways of form and rhetoric. Welcome revolution should not lead us to jettison and forget, as we do so often and so shockingly, many poems and many ways of writing or constituting poems which now seem to us *vieux jeux*. I have always been on the side of revolution and innovation and renewal in the arts, but that should involve examination, constant examination, and evaluation of the traditional as we suppose it to have become.

In the USSR, where it is evident to someone like myself who has no Russian that the arts of poetry have been considered in exceptional depth and richness, revolutionary Vladimir Mayakovsky said that he knew nothing of metre, and cared only for rhythm*—which is the inexplicable, fundamental energy of verse, whatever its depth, whatever the fashions.

G. G.

* *How Verses are Made*, 1926 (tr. G. M. Hyde, 1970)

We Poets in Our Youth

I thought of Chatterton, the marvellous Boy,
The sleepless Soul that perished in his pride;
Of Him who walked in glory and in joy
Following his plough, along the mountain-side:
By our own spirits are we deified:
We Poets in our youth begin in gladness;
But thereof come in the end despondency and madness.

WILLIAM WORDSWORTH

Inscribed in Melrose Abbey

The earth goes on the earth glittering in gold,
The earth goes to the earth sooner than it wold;
The earth builds on the earth castles and towers,
The earth says to the earth, All this is ours.

ANON

The Passing Bell

Come, list and hark, the bell doth toll
For some but now departing soul.
And was not that some ominous fowl—
The bat, the night-crow or the owl?
To these I hear the wild wolf howl
In this black night that seems to scowl.
All these my black-book shall enroll,
For hark! still, still the bell doth toll
For some but now departed soul.

THOMAS HEYWOOD

Upon a Passing Bell

Hark, how the Passing Bell
  Rings out thy neighbour's knell!
And thou, for want of wit
  Or grace, ne'er think'st on it;
Because thou yet art well!

Fool! In two days or three,
  The same may ring for thee!
For Death's impartial dart
  Will surely hit thy heart!
He will not take a fee!

Since, then, he will not spare,
  See thou thyself prepare,
Against that dreadful day,
  When thou shalt turn to clay!
This Bell bids thee, Beware!

THOMAS WASHBOURNE

Hymnus

God be in my hede
  And in my understandyng,
God be in myne eyes
  And in my loking,
God be in my mouth
  And in my speaking,
God be in my harte
  And in my thynkyng,
God be at mine ende
  And at my departyng.

ANON

Time

Time wasteth years, and months, and days, and hours,
 Time doth consume fame, honour, wit, and strength,
Time kills the greenest herbs and sweetest flowers,
 Time wears out youth and beauty's looks at length,
  Time doth convey to ground both foe and friend,
  Ane each thing else but love, which hath no end.

Time maketh every tree to die and rot,
 Time turneth oft our pleasures into pain,
Time causeth wars and wrongs to be forgot,
 Time clears the sky, which first hung full of rain,
  Time makes an end of all humane desire,
  But only this, which sets my heart on fire.

Time turneth into nought each princely state,
 Time brings a flood from new resolved snow,
Time calms the sea where tempest was of late,
 Time eats whate'er the moon can see below;
  And yet no time prevails in my behove,
  Nor any time can make me cease to love:

THOMAS WATSON

Ah! Sun-flower

 Ah, Sun-flower, weary of time,
 Who countest the steps of the Sun,
 Seeking after that sweet golden clime
 Where the traveller's journey is done:

 Where the Youth pined away with desire,
 And the pale Virgin shrouded in snow
 Arise from their graves, and aspire
 Where my Sun-flower wishes to go.

WILLIAM BLAKE

Upon a Funeral

To their long home the greatest princes go
In hearses drest with fair escutcheons round,
The blazons of an ancient race, renown'd
For deeds of valour; and in costly show
The train moves forward in procession slow
Towards some hallow'd Fane; no common ground,
But the arch'd vault and tomb with sculpture crown'd
Receive the corse, with honours laid below.
Alas! whate'er their wealth, their wit, their worth,
Such is the end of all the sons of Earth.

SIR JOHN BEAUMONT

Epitaph of La Graunde Amoure

O mortall folke! you may beholde and se
Howe I lye here, sometime a myghty knyght;
The end of joye and all prosperite
Is deth at last, through his course and myght;
After the day there cometh the derke night;
For though the day be never so longe,
At last the belles ringeth to evensonge.

And my selfe called La Graunde Amoure,
Seking adventure in the worldly glory,
For to attayne the riches and honour,
Did thinke full lytle that I should here lye,
Tyll deth dyde marke me full ryght pryvely.
Lo what I am! and wherto you must!
Lyke as I am so shall you be all dust.

Than in your mynde inwardly despyse
The bryttle worlde, so full of doublenes,
With the vyle flesshe, and ryght sone aryse
Out of your slepe of mortall hevynes;
Subdue the devill with grace and mekenes,
That after your lyfe frayle and transitory,
You may than live in joy perdurably.

STEPHEN HAWES

I Went to Death

"I wende to dede, a king y-wis;
What helps honòur or worldès blis?
Dede is to man the kinde way—
I wende to be clad in clay."

"I wende to dede, clerk ful of skill,
That couthe with wordes men mate and still.
So soone has the dede me made an ende—
Bes war with me! to dede I wende."

"I wende to dede, knight stiff in stowr,
Through fight in feeld I won the flowr.
No fights me taught the dede to quell—
I wende to dede, sooth I you tell."

ANON

dede: death	bes war: beware
y-wis: truly	stiff: strong
couthe: knew (how to)	stowr: battle
mate: subdue	sooth: true
still: silence	

Before Life and After

A time there was—as one may guess
And as, indeed, earth's testimonies tell—
Before the birth of consciousness,
        When all went well.

None suffered sickness, love, or loss,
None knew regret, starved hope, or heart-burnings;
None cared whatever crash or cross
        Brought wrack to things.

If something ceased, no tongue bewailed,
If something winced and waned, no heart was wrung;
If brightness dimmed, and dark prevailed,
        No sense was stung.

But the disease of feeling germed,
And primal rightness took the tinct of wrong;
Ere nescience shall be reaffirmed
How long, how long?

O Blessed Letters

O blessed letters that combine in one
All ages past, and make one live with all,
By you we do confer with who are gone,
And the dead living unto councell call:
By you th'unborne shall have communion
Of what we feele, and what doth us befall.
Soule of the world, knowledge, without thee,
What hath the earth that truly glorious is?
Why should our pride make such a stir to be,
To be forgot? what good is like to this,
To do worthy the writing, and to write
Worthy the reading, and the world's delight?

SAMUEL DANIEL

Verse and Fame

Verse hath a middle nature: heaven keepes Soules,
The Grave keepes bodies, Verse the Fame enroules.

JOHN DONNE

Lying Awake

You, Morningtide Star, now are steady-eyed, over the east,
  I know it as if I saw you;
You, Beeches, engrave on the sky your thin twigs, even the least;
  Had I paper and pencil I'd draw you.

[22]

You, Meadow, are white with your counterpane cover of dew,
   I see it as if I were there;
You, Churchyard, are lightening faint from the shade of the yew,
   The names creeping out everywhere.

THOMAS HARDY

This Life

The lif of this world
   Is ruled with wind,
Weepinge, drede,
   And steryinge:
With wind we blowen,
   With wind we lassen;
With weepinge we comen,
   With weepinge we passen;
With steryinge we beginnen,
   With steryinge we enden;
With drede we dwellen,
   With drede we wenden.

ANON

wind: breathing   dwellen: live
steryinge: commotion   wenden: pass away, depart
blowen: flourish, flower
lassen: fade

The Cherry Fair

Farewell this world! I take my leve for ever;
   I am arrested to appere afore Godes face.
O merciful God, thou knowest that I had lever
   Than all this world to have an houre space
   For to make asseth for my gret trespàce.
      My harte, alas, is broken for that sorrow:
      Some be this day that shall not be to-morow.

This world, I see, is but a chery-fair;
   All thinges passeth, and so moste I algate.
This day I sat full royally in a chair,
   Till sutil deth knokked at my gate,
   And unavised he said to me "chekmate!"
     Lo! how sudeinly he maketh a devorce!
     And, wormes to fede, here he hath laid my corse.

Speke softe, ye folkes, for I am laid aslepe;
   I have my dreme; in trust is muche treason.
From dethes hold fain wold I make a lepe;
   But my wisdom is turned into feble reason.
   I see this worldes joy lasteth but a season;
     Wold God I had remembred this beforne!
     I say no more, but beware of an horne!

This fikel world, so false and so unstable,
   Promoteth his lovers but for a litel while;
But at the last he giveth them a bable,
   When his painted trowth is turned into gile.
   Experience causeth me the trowth to compile,
     Thinking this—too late, alas, that I began!
     For foly and hope disseiveth many a man.

Farewell, my frendes! the tide abideth no man;
   I moste departe hens, and so shall ye.
But in this passage, the best song that I can
   Is *"Requiem Eternam"*: I pray God grant it me.
   When I have ended all myn adversité,
     Grante me in Paradise to have a mansion
     That shede His blode for my redempcion!

ANON

asseth: amends   unavised: with no warning
algate: any way   horne: death's summoning trumpet

A Rueful Lamentation of the Death of Queen Elizabeth, Mother to King Henry VIII

O ye that put your trust and confidence,
In worldly joy and frayle prosperite,
That so lyve here as ye should never hence,
Remember death and loke here uppon me.
Ensaumple I thynke there may no better be.
Your selfe wotte well that in this realme was I,
Your quene but late, and lo now here I lye.

Was I not borne of olde worthy linage?
Was not my mother queene my father kyng?
Was I not a kinges fere in marriage?
Had I not plenty of every pleasaunt thyng?
Merciful God this is a straunge reckenyng:
Rychesse, honour, welth and auncestry
Hath me forsaken and lo now here I ly.

If worship myght have kept me, I had not gone.
If wyt myght have me saved, I neded not fere.
If money myght have holpe, I lacked none.
But O good God what vayleth all this gere.
When deth is come thy mighty messangere,
Obey we must there is no remedy,
Me hath he sommoned, and lo now here I ly.

Yet was I late promised otherwyse,
This yere to live in welth and delice.
Lo where to commeth thy blandishyng promyse,
O false astrolagy and devynatrice,
Of Goddes secretes makyng thy selfe so wyse.
How true is for this yere thy prophecy.
The yere yet lasteth, and lo nowe here I ly.

O bryttill welth, ay full of bitternesse,
Thy single pleasure doubled is with payne.
Account my sorow first and my distresse,
In sondry wyse, and recken there agayne,
The joy that I have had, and I dare sayne,
For all my honour, endured yet have I,
More wo then welth, and lo now here I ly.

Where are our Castels, now where are our Towers,
Goodly Rychmonde sone art thou gone from me,
At Westminster that costly worke of yours,
Myne owne dere lorde now shall I never see.
Almighty God vouchsafe to graunt that ye,
For you and your children well may edefy.
My palyce bylded is, and lo now here I ly.

Adew myne owne dere spouse my worthy lorde,
The faithful love, that dyd us both combyne,
In mariage and peasable concorde,
Into your handes here I cleane resyne,
To be bestowed uppon your children and myne,
Erst wer you father, and now must ye supply
The mothers part also, for lo now here I ly.

Farewell my doughter lady Margarete.
God wotte full oft it greved hath my mynde,
That ye should go where we should seldome mete.
Now am I gone, and have left you behynde.
O mortall folke that we be very blinde.
That we least feare, full oft it is most nye,
From you depart I fyrst, and lo now here I lye.

Farewell Madame my lordes worthy mother,
Comfort your sonne, and be ye of good chere,
Take all a worth, for it will be no nother.
Farewell my doughter Katherine late the fere,
To Prince Arthur myne owne chyld so dere,
It booteth not for me to wepe or cry,
Pray for my soule, for lo now here I ly.

Adew Lord Henry my lovyng sonne adew.
Our lorde encrease your honour and estate,
Adew my doughter Mary bright of hew.
God make you vertuous wyse and fortunate.
Adew swete hart my little doughter Kate,
Thou shalt swete babe suche is thy desteny,
Thy mother never know, for lo now here I ly..

Lady Cicyly Anne and Katheryne.
Farewell my welbeloved sisters three,
O lady Briget other sister myne,
Lo here the ende of worldly vanitee.
Now well are ye that earthly foly flee,
And hevenly thynges love and magnify,
Farewell and pray for me, for lo now here I ly.

Adew my lordes, adew my ladies all,
Adew my faithful servauntes everych one,
Adew my commons whome I never shall,
See in this world wherefore to the alone,
Immortall God verely three and one,
I me commende—thy infinite mercy,
Shew to thy servant, for lo now here I ly.

SIR THOMAS MORE

fere: consort
Take all a worth: take everything patiently, at its worth
commons: folk, people

On the Death of Elizabeth, Queen of Henry VII, and Mother of Henry VIII

Here lith the fresshe flowr of Plantagenet
here lith the white rose in the rede sete
here lith the nobull quen Elyzabeth
here lith the princes departid by deth
here lith blode of owr contray royall
here lith fame of Ynglond immortall

here lith of Edward the IVth a picture
here lith his dowghter and perle pure
here lith the wyff of Harry owr trew kyng
here lith the hart the joy and the gold rynge
here lith the lady so lyberall and gracius
here lith the pleasure of thy hows
here lith very loue of man and child
here lith insampull owre myndez to bild
here lith all bewte of lyvyng a myrrour
here lith all vertu good manner and honour
God grant her now hevyn to encrese
and owr kyng Harry long lyff and pease

ANON

insampull: example

Weep No More

Weep no more, woful Shepherds weep no more,
For *Lycidas* your sorrow is not dead,
Sunk though he be beneath the watry floar,
So sinks the day-star in the Ocean bed,
And yet anon repairs his drooping head,
And tricks his beams, and with new spangled Ore,
Flames in the forehead of the morning sky:
So *Lycidas* sunk low, but mounted high,
Through the dear might of him that walk'd the waves
Where other groves, and other streams along,
With *Nectar* pure his oozy Locks he laves,
And hears the unexpressive nuptiall Song,
In the blest Kingdoms meek of joy and love.
There entertain him all the Saints above,
In solemn troops, and sweet Societies
That sing, and singing in their glory move,
And wipe the tears for ever from his eyes.
Now *Lycidas* the Shepherds weep no more;
Hence forth thou art the Genius of the shore,
In thy large recompense, and shalt be good
To all that wander in that perilous flood.

Thus sang the uncouth Swain to th'Okes and rills,
While the still morn went out with Sandals gray,
He touch'd the tender stops of various Quills,
With eager thought warbling his *Dorick* lay:
And now the Sun had stretch'd out all the hills,
And now was dropt into the Western bay;
At last he rose, and twitch'd his Mantle blew:
To-morrow to fresh Woods, and Pastures new.

JOHN MILTON

The Timber

Sure thou didst flourish once! and many Springs,
Many bright mornings, much dew, many showers
Past ore thy head: many light *Hearts* and *Wings*
Which now are dead, lodg'd in thy living bowers.

And still a new succession sings and flies;
Fresh Groves grow up, and their green branches shoot
Towards the old and still enduring skies,
While the low *Violet* thrives at their root.

But thou beneath the sad and heavy *Line*
Of death, dost waste all senseless, cold and dark;
Where not so much as dreams of light may shine;
Nor any thought of greenness, leaf or bark.

And yet (as if some deep hate and dissent,
Bred in thy growth betwixt high winds and thee,
Were still alive) thou dost great storms resent
Before they come, and know'st how near they be.

Else all at rest thou lyest, and the fierce breath
Of tempests can no more disturb thy ease;
But this thy strange resentment after death
Means onely those, who broke (in life) thy peace.

So murthered man, when lovely life is done,
And his blood freez'd, keeps in the Center still
Some secret sense, which makes the dead blood run
At his approach, that did the body kill.

And is there any murth'rer worse then sin?
Or any storms more foul then a lewd life?
Or what *Resentient* can work more within,
Then true remorse, when with past sins at strife?

He that hath left lifes vain joys and vain care,
And truly hates to be detain'd on earth,
Hath got an house where many mansions are,
And keeps his soul unto eternal mirth.

But though thus dead unto the world, and ceas'd
From sin, he walks a narrow, private way;
Yet grief and old wounds make him sore displeas'd,
And all his life a rainy, weeping day. . . .

HENRY VAUGHAN

Inscription Above the Entrance
to the Abbey of Theleme

Here enter not vile bigots, hypocrites,
Externally devoted Apes, base snites,
Puft up, wry-necked beasts, worse than the Huns
Or Ostrogots, forerunners of baboons:
Curst snakes, dissembled varlets, seeming Sancts,
Slipshod caffards, beggars pretending wants,
Fat chuff-cats, smell-feast knockers, doltish gulls,
Out-strouting cluster-fists, contentious bulls,
Fomenters of divisions and debates,
Elsewhere, not here, make sale of your deceits.

Your filthy trumperies
Stuff't with pernicious lies,
    (Not worth a bubble)
    Would do but trouble
Our earthly Paradise,
Your filthy trumperies.

Here enter not Attorneys, Barristers,
Nor bridle-champing law-Practitioners:
Clerks, Commissaries, Scribes nor Pharisees,
Wilful disturbers of the People's ease:
Judges, destroyers, with an unjust breath,
Of honest men, like dogs, ev'n unto death.
Your salary is at the gibbet-foot:
Go drink there; for we do not here fly out
On those excessive courses, which may draw
A waiting on your courts by suits in law.

    Lawsuits, debates and wrangling
    Hence are exil'd, and jangling
        Here we are very
        Frolick and merry,
    And free from all entangling,
    Lawsuits, debates and wrangling.

Here enter not base pinching Usurers,
Pelf-lickers, everlasting gatherers.
Gold-graspers, coin-gripers, gulpers of mists:
Niggish deformed sots, who, though your chests
Vast sums of money should to you afford,
Would ne'er the less add more unto that hoard,
And yet be not content, you cluntchfist dastards,
Insatiable fiends, and Pluto's bastards.
Greedy devourers, chichie sneakbill rogues,
Hell-mastiffs gnaw your bones, you rav'nous dogs.

You beastly looking fellows,
Reason doth plainly tell us,
    That we should not
    To you allot
Room here, but at the gallows,
You beastly looking fellows.

Here enter not fond makers of demurs
In love adventures, peevish, jealous curs.
Sad pensive dotards, raisers of garboils,
Hags, goblins, ghosts, firebrands of household broils.
Nor drunkards, liars, cowards, cheaters, clowns,
Thieves, cannibals, faces o'ercast with frowns.
Nor lazy slugs, envious, covetous:
Nor blockish, cruel, nor too credulous.
Here mangy, pocky folks shall have no place,
No ugly lusks, nor persons of disgrace.

    Grace, honour, praise, delight,
    Here sojourn day and night.
        Sound bodies lin'd
        With a good mind,
    Do here pursue with might
    Grace, honour, praise, delight.

Here enter you, and welcome from our hearts,
All noble sparks, endow'd with gallant parts.
This is the glorious place, which bravely shall
Afford wherewith to entertain you all.
Were you a thousand, here you shall not want
For any thing; for what you'll ask, we'll grant.
Stay here, you lively, jovial, handsome, brisk,
Gay, witty, frolic, cheerful, merry, frisk,
Spruce, jocund, courteous, furtherers of trades,
And, in a word, all worthy gentile blades.

Blades of heroic breasts
Shall taste here of the feasts,
  Both privily
  And civily
Of the celestial guests,
Blades of heroic breasts.

Here enter you, pure, honest, faithful, true,
Expounders of the Scriptures old and new.
Whose glosses do not blind our reason, but
Make it to see the clearer, and who shut
Its passages from hatred, avarice,
Pride, factions, cov'nants, and all sort of vice.
Come, settle here a charitable faith,
Which neighbourly affection nourisheth.
And whose light chaseth all corrupters hence,
Of the blest Word, from the aforesaid sense.

  The Holy Sacred Word
  May it always afford
    T'us all in common
    Both man and woman
  A sp'ritual shield and sword,
  The Holy Sacred Word.

Here enter you all Ladies of high birth,
Delicious, stately, charming, full of mirth,
Ingenious, lovely, miniard, proper, fair,
Magnetic, graceful, splendid, pleasant, rare,
Obliging, sprightly, virtuous, young, solacious,
Kind, neat, quick, feat, bright, compt, ripe, choice, dear, precious.
Alluring, courtly, comely, fine, complete,
Wise, personable, ravishing and sweet.
Come joys enjoy, the Lord Celestial
Hath giv'n enough, wherewith to please us all.

Gold give us, God forgive us,
And from all woes relieve us.
That we the treasure
May reap of pleasure.
And shun what e'er is grievous.
Gold give us, God forgive us.

SIR THOMAS URQUHART
(*after* Rabelais)

The Soul's Calm Sunshine

What nothing earthly gives, or can destroy
The soul's calm sunshine, and the heart-felt joy,
Is Virtue's prize: A better would you fix?
Then give Humility a coach and six,
Justice a Conq'r's sword, or Truth a gown,
Or Public Spirit it great cure, a Crown.
Weak, foolish man! will Heav'n reward us there
With the same trash mad mortals wish for here?
The Boy and Man an individual makes,
Yet sigh'st thou now for apples and for cakes?

ALEXANDER POPE

Abou Ben Adhem and the Angel

Abou Ben Adhem (may his tribe increase)
Awoke one night from a deep dream of peace,
And saw, within the moonlight in his room,
Making it rich, and like a lily in bloom,
An angel writing in a book of gold:—
Exceeding peace had made Ben Adhem bold,
And to the presence in the room he said,
"What writest thou?"—The vision rais'd its head,
And with a look made of all sweet accord,
Answer'd, "The names of those who love the Lord."
"And is mine one?" said Abou. "Nay, not so,"

Replied the angel. Abou spoke more low,
But cheerly still; and said, "I pray thee then,
"Write me as one that loves his fellow men."

The angel wrote, and vanish'd. The next night.
It came again with a great wakening light,
And show'd the names whom love of God had bless'd,
And lo! Ben Adhem's, name led all the rest.*

LEIGH HUNT

* "On rapporte de lui (Abou-Ishak-Ben-Adhem), qu'il vit en songe
un ange qui écrivoit, et que lui ayant demandé ce qu'il faisoit, cet ange
lui répondit: "J'écris le nom de ceux qui aiment sincèrement Dieu, tels
que sont Malek-Ben-Dinar, Thaber-al-Benani, Aioud-al-Sakhtiani,
etc." Alors il dit à l'ange, "Ne suis-je point parmi ces
gens-là?"—"Non," lui répondit l'ange. "Hé bien," répliqua-t-il,
"écrivez-moi, je vous prie, pour l'amour d'eux, en qualité d'ami de
ceux qui aiment Dieu." L'on ajoute, que le même ange lui révéla
bientôt après, qu'il avoit reçu ordre de Dieu de le mettre à la tête de
tous les autres." D'Herbelot—*Bibliothèque Orientale*, 1781. Tom. i.
p. 161. in voc. *Adhem*.

Le Vallon

Mon cœur lassé de tout, même de l'espérance,
N'ira plus de ses vœux importuner le sort;
Prêtez-moi seulement, vallons de mon enfance,
Un asile d'un jour pour attendre la mort.

Voici l'étroit sentier de l'obscure vallée;
Du flanc de ces coteaux pendent des bois épais,
Qui, courbant sur mon front leur ombre entremêlée,
Me couvrent tout entier de silence et de paix.

Là deux ruisseaux cachés sous des ponts de verdure
Tracent en serpentant les contours du vallon;
Ils mêlent un moment leur onde et leur murmure,
Et non loin de leur source ils se perdent sans nom.

La source de mes jours comme eux s'est écoulée;
Elle a passé sans bruit, sans nom et sans retour;
Mais leur onde est limpide, et mon âme troublée
N'aura pas réfléchi les clartés d'un beau jour.

La fraîcheur de leurs lits, l'ombre qui les couronne,
M'enchaînent tout le jour sur les bords des ruisseaux;
Comme un enfant bercé par un chant monotone
Mon âme s'assoupit au murmure des eaux.

Ah! c'est là qu'entouré d'un rempart de verdure,
D'un horizon borné qui suffit à mes yeux,
J'aime à fixer mes pas, et seul dans la nature,
A n'entendre que l'onde, à ne voir que les cieux.

J'ai trop vu, trop senti, trop aimé dans ma vie;
Je viens chercher vivant le calme du Léthé.
Beaux lieux soyez pour moi ces bords où l'on oublie
L'oubli seul désormais est ma félicité.

Mon cœur est en repos, mon âme est en silence;
Le bruit lointain du monde expire en arrivant,
Comme un son éloigné qu'affaiblit la distance,
A l'oreille incertaine apporté par le vent.

D'ici je vois la vie, à travers un nuage,
S'évanouir pour moi dans l'ombre du passé
L'amour seul est resté, comme une grande image
Survit seul au réveil dans un songe effacé.

Repose-toi, mon âme, en ce dernier asile,
Ainsi qu'un voyageur qui, le cœur plein d'espoir,
S'assied, avant d'entrer, aux portes de la ville,
Et respire un moment l'air embaumé du soir.

Comme lui, de nos pieds secouant la poussière;
L'homme par ce chemin ne repasse jamais
Comme lui, respirons au bout de la carrière
Ce calme avant-coureur de l'éternelle paix.

Tes jours sombres et courts comme les jours d'automne
Déclinent comme l'ombre au penchant des coteaux
L'amitié te trahit, la pitié t'abandonne,
Et, seule, tu descends le sentier des tombeaux.

Mais la nature est là qui t'invite et qui t'aime;
Plonge-toi dans son sein qu'elle t'ouvre toujours;
Quand tout change pour toi, la nature est la même,
Et le même soleil se lève sur tes jours.

De lumière et d'ombrage elle t'entoure encore;
Détache ton amour des faux biens que tu perds;
Adore ici l'écho qu'adorait Pythagore,
Prête avec lui l'oreille aux célestes concerts.

Suis le jour dans le ciel, suis l'ombre sur la terre;
Dans les plaines de l'air vole avec l'aquilon;
Avec le doux rayon de l'astre du mystère
Glisse à travers les bois dans l'ombre du vallon.

Dieu pour le concevoir a fait l'intelligence:
Sous la nature enfin découvre son auteur.
Une voix à l'esprit parle dans son silence;
Qui n'a pas entendu cette voix dans son cœur?

ALPHONSE DE LAMARTINE

I Was a Stricken Deer

I was a stricken deer, that left the herd
Long since; with many an arrow deep infixt
My panting side was charg'd, when I withdrew
To seek a tranquil death in distant shades.
There was I found by one who had himself
Been hurt by th'archers. In his side he bore,
And in his hands and feet, the cruel scars.
With gentle force soliciting the darts,
He drew them forth, and heal'd, and bade me live.
Since then, with few associates, in remote
And silent woods I wander, far from those
My former partners of the peopled scene;
With few associates, and not wishing more.
Here much I ruminate, as much I may,
With other views of men and manners now

Than once, and others of a life to come.
I see that all are wand'rers, gone astray
Each in his own delusions; they are lost
In chase of fancied happiness, still woo'd
And never won. Dream after dream ensues;
And still they dream that they shall still succeed.
And still are disappointed. Rings the world
With the vain stir. I sum up half mankind,
And add two-thirds of the remaining half,
And find the total of their hopes and fears
Dreams, empty dreams. The million flit as gay
As if created only like the fly,
That spreads his motley wings in th' eye of noon,
To sport their season, and be seen no more.

WILLIAM COWPER

To an Unborn Pauper Child

I

Breathe not, hid Heart: cease silently,
And though thy birth-hour beckons thee,
    Sleep the long sleep:
    The Doomsters heap
Travails and teens around us here,
And Time-wraiths turn our songsingings to fear.

II

Hark, how the peoples surge and sigh,
And laughters fail, and greetings die:
    Hopes dwindle; yea,
    Faiths waste away,
Affections and enthusiasms numb;
Thou canst not mend these things if thou dost come.

III

Had I the ear of wombèd souls
Ere their terrestrial chart unrolls,
    And thou wert free
    To cease, or be,
Then would I tell thee all I know,
And put it to thee: Wilt thou take Life so?

IV

Vain vow! No hint of mine may hence
To theeward fly: to thy locked sense
    Explain none can
    Life's pending plan:
Thou wilt thy ignorant entry make
Though skies spout fire and blood and nations quake.

V

Fain would I, dear, find some shut plot
Of earth's wide wold for thee, where not
    One tear, one qualm,
    Should break the calm.
But I am weak as thou and bare;
No man can change the common lot to rare.

VI

Must come and bide. And such are we—
Unreasoning, sanguine, visionary—
    That I can hope
    Health, love, friends, scope
In full for thee; can dream thou'lt find
Joys seldom yet attained by humankind!

THOMAS HARDY

Afterwards

When the Present has latched its postern behind my tremulous stay,
    And the May month flaps its glad green leaves like wings,
Delicate-filmed as new-spun silk, will the neighbours say,
    "He was a man who used to notice such things"?

[39]

If it be in the dusk when, like an eyelid's soundless blink,
  The dewfall-hawk comes crossing the shades to alight
Upon the wind-warped upland thorn, a gazer may think,
  "To him this must have been a familiar sight."

If I pass during some nocturnal blackness, mothy and warm,
  When the hedgehog travels furtively over the lawn,
One may say, "He strove that such innocent creatures should come to
    no harm,
  But he could do little for them; and now he is gone."

If, when hearing that I have been stilled at last, they stand at the door,
  Watching the full-starred heavens that winter sees,
Will this thought rise on those who will meet my face no more,
  "He was one who had an eye for such mysteries"?

And will any say when my bell of quittance is heard in the gloom,
  And a crossing breeze cuts a pause in its outrollings,
Till they rise again, as they were a new bell's boom,
  "He hears it not now, but used to notice such things"?

THOMAS HARDY

Lausanne
In Gibbon's Old Garden: 11–12 p.m.
June 27, 1897

The 110th anniversary of the
completion of the *Decline and Fall*
at the same hour and place

A spirit seems to pass,
  Formal in pose, but grave withal and grand:
  He contemplates a volume in his hand,
And far lamps fleck him through the thin acacias.

Anon the book is closed,
  With "It is finished!" And at the alley's end
  He turns, and when on me his glances bend
As from the Past comes speech—small, muted, yet composed.

[40]

"How fares the Truth now?—Ill?
—Do pens but slily further her advance?
May one not speed her but in phrase askance?
Do scribes aver the Comic to be Reverend still?

"Still rule those minds on earth
At whom sage Milton's wormwood words were hurled:
'Truth like a bastard comes into the world
Never without ill-fame to him who gives her birth'?"

THOMAS HARDY

Friends Beyond

William Dewy, Tranter Reuben, Farmer Ledlow late at plough,
    Robert's kin, and John's, and Ned's,
And the Squire, and Lady Susan, lie in Mellstock churchyard now!

"Gone," I call them, gone for good, that group of local hearts and
        heads;
    Yet at mothy curfew-tide,
And at midnight when the noon-heat breathes it back from walls and
        leads,

They've a way of whispering to me—fellow-wight who yet abide—
    In the muted, measured note
Of a ripple under archways, or a lone cave's stillicide:

"We have triumphed: this achievement turns the bane to antidote,
    Unsuccesses to success,
Many thought-worn eves and morrows to a morrow free of thought.

"No more need we corn and clothing, feel of old terrestrial stress;
    Chill detraction stirs no sigh;
Fear of death has even bygone us: death gave all that we possess."

W.D.:   "Ye mid burn the old bass-viol that I set such value by."
SQUIRE: "You may hold the manse in fee,
              You may wed my spouse, may let my children's memory
                    of me die."

[41]

LADY S.! "You may have my rich brocades, my laces; take each
            household key;
            Ransack coffer, desk, bureau;
            Quiz the few poor treasures hid there, con the letters kept
            by me."

FAR.:   "Ye mid zell my favourite heifer, ye mid let the charlock
            grow,
            Foul the grinterns, give up thrift."
FAR. WIFE: "If ye break my best blue china, children, I shan't care or
            ho."

ALL: "We've no wish to hear the tidings, how the people's
            fortunes shift;
            What your daily doings are;
            Who are wedded, born, divided; if your lives beat slow or
            swift.

"Curious not the least are we if our intents you make or mar,
    If you quire to our old tune,
If the City stage still passes, if the weirs still roar afar."

—Thus, with very gods' composure, freed those crosses late and soon
    Which, in my life, the Trine allow
(Why, none witteth), and ignore all that haps beneath the moon,

William Dewy, Tranter Reuben, Farmer Ledlow late at plough,
    Robert's kin, and John's, and Ned's,
And the Squire, and Lady Susan, murmur mildly to me now.

                                            THOMAS HARDY

[42]

Epitaph

I never cared for Life: Life cared for me,
And hence I owed it some fidelity.
It now says, "Cease; at length thou hast learnt to grind
Sufficient toll for an unwilling mind,
And I dismiss thee—not without regard
That thou didst ask no ill-advised reward,
Nor sought in me much more than thou couldst find."

THOMAS HARDY

Old Counsel
Of the Young Master of a Wrecked
California Clipper

Come out of the Golden Gate,
Go round the Horn with streamers,
Carry royals early and late;
But, brother, be not over-elate—
All hands save ship! has startled dreamers.

HERMAN MELVILLE

The Deserter's Lamentation

If sadly thinking,
And spirits sinking,
Could more than drinking
    Our griefs compose—
A cure for sorrow
From care I'd borrow;
And hope tomorrow
    Might end my woes.

But since in wailing
There's naught availing,
For Death, unfailing,
  Will strike the blow;
Then, for that reason,
And for the season,
Let us be merry
  Before we go!

A wayworn ranger,
To joy a stranger,
Through every danger
  My course I've run.
Now, death befriending,
His last aid lending,
My griefs are ending,
  My woes are done.

No more a rover,
Or hapless lover,
Those cares are over—
  "My cup runs low";
Then, for that reason,
And for the season,
Let us be merry
Before we go!

JOHN PHILPOT CURRAN

The Climb to Snowdon

In one of these excursions, travelling then
Through Wales on foot, and with a youthful Friend,
I left Bethhelert's huts at couching-time,
And westward took my way to see the sun
Rise from the top of Snowdon. Having reach'd
The Cottage at the Mountain's foot, we there
Rouz'd up the Shepherd, who by ancient right
Of office is the Stranger's usual guide;
And after short refreshment sallied forth.

It was a Summer's night, a close warm night,
Wan, dull and glaring, with a dripping mist
Low-hung and thick that cover'd all the sky,
Half threatening storm and rain; but on we went
Uncheck'd, being full of heart and having faith
In our tried Pilot. Little could we see
Hemm'd round on every side with fog and damp,
And, after ordinary travellers' chat
With our Conductor, silently we sank
Each into commerce with his private thoughts:
Thus did we breast the ascent, and by myself
Was nothing either seen or heard the while
Which took me from my musings, save that once
The Shepherd's Cur did to his own great joy
Unearth a hedgehog in the mountain crags
Round which he made a barking turbulent.
This small adventure, for even such it seemed
In that wild place and at the dead of night,
Being over and forgotten, on we wound
In silence as before. With forehead bent
Earthward, as if in opposition set
Against an enemy, I panted up
With eager pace, and no less eager thoughts.
Thus might we wear perhaps an hour away,
Ascending at loose distance each from each,
And I, as chanced, the foremost of the Band;
When at my feet the ground appear'd to brighten,
And with a step or two seem'd brighter still;
Nor had I time to ask the cause of this,
For instantly a Light upon the turf
Fell like a flash: I looked about, and lo!
The Moon stood naked in the Heavens, at height
Immense above my head, and on the shore
I found myself of a huge sea of mist,
Which, meek and silent, rested at my feet:
A hundred hills their dusky backs upheaved
All over this still Ocean, and beyond,
Far, far beyond, the vapours shot themselves,
In headlands, tongues, and promontory shapes,
In the Sea, the real Sea, that seem'd

[45]

To dwindle, and give up its majesty,
Usurp'd upon as far as sight could reach.
Meanwhile, the Moon look'd down upon this shew
In single glory, and we stood, the mist
Touching our very feet; and from the shore
At distance not the third part of a mile
Was a blue chasm; a fracture in the vapour,
A deep and gloomy breathing-place through which
Mounted the roar of waters, torrents, streams
Innumerable, roaring with one voice.
The universal spectacle throughout
Was shaped for admiration and delight,
Grand in itself alone, but in that breach
Through which the homeless voice of waters rose,
That dark deep thoroughfare had Nature lodg'd
The Soul, the Imagination of the whole.

   A meditation rose in me that night
Upon the lonely Mountains when the scene
Had pass'd away, and it appear'd to me
The perfect image of a mighty Mind,
Of one that feeds upon infinity,
That is exalted by an underpresence,
The sense of God, or whatsoe'er is dim
Or vast in its own being, above all
One function of such mind had Nature there
Exhibited by putting forth, and that
With circumstance most awful and sublime,
That domination which she oftentimes
Exerts upon the outward face of things,
So moulds them, and endues, abstracts, combines,
Or by abrupt and unhabitual influence
Doth make one object so impress itself
Upon all others, and pervade them so
That even the grossest minds must see and hear
And cannot chuse but feel. The Power which these
Acknowledge when thus moved, which Nature thus
Thrusts forth upon the senses, is the express
Resemblance, in the fulness of its strength
Made visible, a genuine Counterpart

And Brother of the glorious faculty
Which higher minds bear with them as their own.
That is the very spirit in which they deal
With all the objects of the universe;
They from their native selves can send abroad
Like transformations, for themselves create
A like existence, and, whene'er it is
Created for them, catch it by an instinct;
Them the enduring and the transient both
Serve to exalt; they build up greatest things
From least suggestions, ever on the watch,
Willing to work and to be wrought upon,
They need not extraordinary calls
To rouze them, in a world of life they live,
By sensible impressions not enthrall'd,
But quicken'd, rouz'd and made thereby more apt
To hold communion with the invisible world.
Such minds are truly from the Deity,
For they are Powers; and hence the highest bliss
That can be known is theirs, the consciousness
Of whom they are habitually infused
Through every image, and through every thought,
And all impressions; hence religion, faith,
And endless occupation for the soul
Whether discursive or intuitive;
Hence sovereignty within and peace at will
Emotion which best foresight need not fear
Most worthy then of trust when most intense.
Hence chearfulness in every act of life
Hence truth in moral judgements and delight
That fails not in the external universe.

   Oh! who is he that hath his whole life long
Preserved, enlarged, this freedom in himself?
For this alone is genuine Liberty:
Witness, ye Solitudes! where I received
My earliest visitations, careless then
Of what was given me, and where now I roam,
A meditative, oft a suffering Man,
And yet, I trust, with undiminish'd powers,

Witness, whatever falls my better mind,
Revolving with the accidents of life,
May have sustain'd, that, howsoe'er misled,
I never, in the quest of right and wrong,
Did tamper with myself from private aims;
Nor was in any of my hopes the dupe
Of selfish passions; nor did wilfully
Yield ever to mean cares and low pursuits;
But rather did with jealousy shrink back
From every combination that might aid
The tendency, too potent in itself,
Of habit to enslave the mind, I mean
Oppress it by the laws of vulgar sense,
And substitute a universe of death,
The falsest of all worlds, in place of that
Which is divine and true. To fear and love,
To love as first and chief, for there fear ends,
Be this ascribed; to early intercourse,
In presence of sublime and lovely forms,
With the adverse principles of pain and joy,
Evil as one is rashly named by those
Who know not what they say. By love, for here
Do we begin and end, all grandeur comes,
All truth and beauty, from pervading love,
That gone, we are as dust. Behold the fields
In balmy spring-time, full of rising flowers
And happy creatures; see that Pair, the Lamb
And the Lamb's Mother, and their tender ways
Shall touch thee to the heart; in some green bower
Rest, and be not alone, but have thou there
The One who is thy choice of all the world,
There linger, lull'd and lost, and rapt away,
Be happy to thy fill; thou call'st this love
And so it is, but there is higher love
Than this, a love that comes into the heart
With awe and a diffusive sentiment;
Thy love is human merely; this proceeds
More from the brooding Soul, and is divine.

This love more intellectual cannot be
Without Imagination, which, in truth,
Is but another name for absolute strength
And clearest insight, amplitude of mind,
And reason in her most exalted mood.
This faculty hath been the moving soul
Of our long labour: we have traced the stream
From darkness, and the very place of birth
In its blind cavern, whence is faintly heard
The sound of waters; follow'd it to light
And open day, accompanied its course
Among the ways of Nature, afterwards
Lost sight of it bewilder'd and engulph'd,
Then given it greeting, as it rose once more
With strength, reflecting in its solemn breast
The works of man and face of human life,
And lastly, from its progress have we drawn
The feeling of life endless, the great thought
By which we live, Infinity and God.
Imagination having been our theme,
So also hath that intellectual love,
For they are each in each, and cannot stand
Dividually.—Here must thou be, O Man!
Strength to thyself; no Helper hast thou here;
Here keepest thou thy individual state:
No other can divide with thee this work,
No secondary hand can intervene
To fashion this ability; 'tis thine,
The prime and vital principle is thine
In the recesses of thy nature, far
From any reach of outward fellowship,
Else is not thine at all. But joy to him,
Oh, joy to him who here hath sown, hath laid
Here the foundations of his future years!
For all that friendship, all that love can do,
All that a darling countenance can look
Or dear voice utter to complete the man,
Perfect him, made imperfect in himself,
All shall be his: and he whose soul hath risen
Up to the height of feeling intellect

Shall want no humbler tenderness, his heart
Be tender as a nursing Mother's heart;
Of female softness shall his life be full,
Of little loves and delicate desires,
Mild interests and gentlest sympathies.

　　Child of my Parents! Sister of my Soul!
Elsewhere have streams of gratitude been breath'd
To thee for all the early tenderness
Which I from thee imbibed. And true it is
That later seasons owed to thee no less;
For, spite of thy sweet influence and the touch
Of other kindred hands that open'd out
The springs of tender thought in infancy,
And spite of all which singly I had watch'd
Of elegance, and each minuter charm
In nature and in life, still to the last
Even to the very going out of youth,
The period which our Story now hath reach'd,
I too exclusively esteem'd that love,
And sought that beauty, which, as Milton sings,
Hath terror in it. Thou didst soften down
This over-sternness; but for thee, sweet Friend,
My soul, too reckless of mild grace, had been
Far longer what by Nature it was framed,
Longer retain'd its countenance severe,
A rock with torrents roaring, with the clouds
Familiar, and a favourite of the Stars:
But thou didst plant its crevices with flowers,
Hang it with shrubs that twinkle in the breeze,
And teach the little birds to build their nests
And warble in its chambers. At a time
When Nature, destined to remain so long
Foremost in my affections, had fallen back
Into a second place, well pleas'd to be
A handmaid to a nobler than herself,
When every day brought with it some new sense
Of exquisite regard for common things,
And all the earth was budding with these gifts
Of more refined humanity, thy breath,

Dear Sister, was a kind of gentler spring
That went before my steps.

                      With such a theme,
Coleridge! with this my argument, of thee
Shall I be silent? O most loving Soul!
Placed on this earth to love and understand,
And from thy presence shed the light of love,
Shall I be mute ere thou be spoken of?
Thy gentle Spirit to my heart of hearts
Did also find its way; and thus the life
Of all things and the mighty unity
In all which we behold, and feel, and are,
Admitted more habitually a mild
Interposition, and closelier gathering thoughts
Of man and his concerns, such as become
A human Creature, be he who he may!
Poet, or destined for a humbler name;
And so the deep enthusiastic joy,
The rapture of the Hallelujah sent
From all that breathes and is, was chasten'd, stemm'd
And balanced by a Reason which indeed
Is reason; duty and pathetic truth;
And God and Man divided, as they ought,
Between them the great system of the world
Where Man is sphered, and which God animates.

WILLIAM WORDSWORTH

To the Evening Star

Thou fair-hair'd angel of the evening,
Now, whilst the sun rests on the moutains, light
Thy bright torch of love; thy radiant crown
Put on, and smile upon our evening bed!
Smile on our loves, and, while thou drawest the
Blue curtains of the sky, scatter thy silver dew
On every flower that shuts its sweet eyes
In timely sleep. Let thy west wind sleep on
The lake; speak silence with thy glimmering eyes,

And wash the dusk with silver. Soon, full soon,
Dost thou withdraw; then the wolf rages wide,
And the lion glares thro' the dun forest:
The fleeces of our flocks are cover'd with
Thy sacred dew: protect them with thine influence.

WILLIAM BLAKE

Dover Beach

The sea is calm to-night.
The tide is full, the moon lies fair
Upon the straits;—on the French coast the light
Gleams and is gone; the cliffs of England stand,
Glimmering and vast, out in the tranquil bay.
Come to the window, sweet is the night-air!
Only, from the long line of spray
Where the sea meets the moon-blanched land,
Listen! you hear the grating roar
Of pebbles which the waves draw back, and fling,
At their return, up the high strand,
Begin, and cease, and then again begin,
With tremulous cadence slow, and bring
The eternal note of sadness in.

Sophocles long ago
Heard it on the Ægæan, and it brought
Into his mind the turbid ebb and flow
Of human misery; we
Find also in the sound a thought,
Hearing it by this distant northern sea.

The Sea of Faith
Was once, too, at the full, and round earth's shore
Lay like the folds of a bright girdle furled.
But now I only hear
Its melancholy, long, withdrawing roar,
Retreating, to the breath
Of the night-wind, down the vast edges drear
And naked shingles of the world.

Ah, love, let us be true
To one another! for the world, which seems
To lie before us like a land of dreams,
So various, so beautiful, so new,
Hath really neither joy, nor love, nor light,
Nor certitude, nor peace, nor help for pain;
And we are here as on a darkling plain
Swept with confused alarms of struggle and flight,
Where ignorant armies clash by night.

MATTHEW ARNOLD

Not Here, O Apollo

Through the black, rushing smoke-bursts,
Thick breaks the red flame;
All Etna heaves fiercely
Her forest-clothed frame.

Not here, O Apollo!
Are haunts meet for thee.
But, where Helicon breaks down
In cliff to the sea,

Where the moon-silvered inlets
Send far their light voice
Up the still vale of Thisbe,
O speed, and rejoice!

On the sward at the cliff-top
Lie strewn the white flocks,
On the cliff-side the pigeons
Roost deep in the rocks.

In the moonlight the shepherds
Soft lulled by the rills,
Lie wrapped in their blankets
Asleep on the hills.

—What forms are these coming
So white through the gloom?
What garments out-glistening
The gold-flowered broom?

What sweet-breathing presence
Out-perfumes the thyme?
What voices enrapture
The night's balmy prime?

'Tis Apollo comes leading
His choir, the Nine.
—The leader is fairest,
But all are divine.

They are lost in the hollows!
They stream up again!
What seeks on this mountain
The glorified train?

They bathe on this mountain,
In the spring by their road;
Then on to Olympus,
Their endless abode.

—Whose praise do they mention?
Of what is it told?
What will be for ever;
What was from of old.

First hymn they the Father
Of all things; and then,
The rest of immortals,
The action of men.

The day in his hotness,
The strife with the palm;
The night in her silence,
The stars in their calm.

MATTHEW ARNOLD

[54]

How Sweet the Moonlight
Sleeps upon this Bank

How sweet the moonlight sleeps upon this bank!
Here will we sit and let the sounds of music
Creep in our ears; soft stillness and the night
Become the touches of sweet harmony.
Sit, Jessica. Look how the floor of heaven
Is thick inlaid with patens of bright gold.
There's not the smallest orb which thou behold'st
But in his motion like an angel sings,
Still quiring to the young-eyed cherubins;
Such harmony is in immortal souls,
But whilst this muddy vesture of decay
Doth grossly close it in, we cannot hear it.
(*Enter Musicians.*)
Come ho, and wake Diana with a hymn!
With sweetest touches pierce your mistress' ear
And draw her home with music.

WILLIAM SHAKESPEARE

O Sweet Woods

O sweet woods the delight of solitarines!
O how much I do like your solitarines!
Where man's mind hath a freed consideration
Of goodnes to receive lovely direction.
Where senses do behold th'order of heav'nly hoste,
And wise thoughts do behold what the creator is:
Contemplation here holdeth his only seate:
Bownded with no limitts, borne with a wing of hope
Clymes even unto the starres, Nature is under it.
Nought disturbs thy quiet, all to thy service yeeld,
Each sight draws on a thought, thought mother of science,
Sweet birds kindly do graunt harmony unto thee,
Faire trees' shade is enough fortification,
Nor danger to thy selfe if be not in thy selfe.

O sweete woods the delight of solitarines!
O how much I do like your solitarines!
Here no treason is hidd, vailed in innocence,
Nor envie's snaky ey, finds any harbor here,
Nor flatterers' venomous insinuations,
Nor conning humorists' puddled opinions,
Nor courteous ruin of proffered usury,
Nor time pratled away, cradle of ignorance,
Nor causelesse duty, nor comber of arrogance,
Nor trifling title of vanity dazleth us,
Nor golden manacles, stand for a paradise,
Here wrong's name is unheard: slander a monster is.
Keepe thy sprite from abuse, here no abuse doth haunte.
What man grafts in a tree dissimulation?

O sweete woods the delight of solitarines!
O how well I do like your solitarines!
Yet deare soile, if a soule closed in a mansion
As sweete as violetts, faire as a lilly is,
Streight as Cedar, a voice staines the Cannary birds,
Whose shade safety doth hold, danger avoideth her:
Such wisedome, that in her lives speculation:
Such goodnes that in her simplicitie triumphs:
Where envie's snaky ey, winketh or els dyeth,
Slander wants a pretext, flattery gone beyond:
Oh! if such a one have bent to a lonely life
Her stepps, gladd we receave, gladd we receave her eys.
  And thinke not she doth hurt our solitarines,
  For such company decks such solitarines.

SIR PHILIP SIDNEY

Spring: a Formal Ode

Wrinkled, but not inured by years,
Deceived by men, unmanned by fate,
By all that subjugates the mind
Or leaves the heart disconsolate,
However you may bear defeat
Or wrongs, in recollection, sting—
What can withstand the subtle breath
And first encounter of the spring?

Her laws are wayward, self-decreed,
Winged visitant whom none may sue—
The hour appointed, she descends
Unconscious of your woes and you:
No wrinkle in that shining, calm
Forehead of immortality,
Whose lucence and indifference
Befit the brow of deity.

As though it were the first of springs,
She scatters round her fresh increase;
If other springs have ventured here,
No recollection breaks their peace:
She does not care: she only knows
These clouds are hers that sail so wide:
If flowers have shrivelled here before,
Her memory of that death has died.

Past being does not stir the rose
Nor Philomela with its fears;
Not for the past Aurora sheds
Her fragrant, aromatic tears;
Their life, an ocean without bound.
No dread of what is yet to be
Invades this present certitude
Diffused by every leaf and tree.

Accept the absolute decree.
The senses tell you of decay?
Plunge deeper than their knowledge dares
When deity has led the way:
Entering this reviving stream,
Wash wounds beneath the season's spate,
And, though they be the moment's gift,
Among these quickening joys participate.

FYODOR TYUCHEV
(translated from the Russian
by Charles Tomlinson)

The Flower

How fresh, O Lord, how sweet and clean
Are thy returns! ev'n as the flowers in spring;
To which, besides their own demean,
The late-past frosts tributes of pleasure bring.
Grief melts away
Like snow in May,
As if there were no such cold thing.

Who would have thought my shrivel'd heart
Could have recover'd greennesse? It was gone
Quite under ground; as flowers depart
To see their mother-root, when they have blown;
Where they together
All the hard weather,
Dead to the world, keep house unknown.

These are thy wonders, Lord of power,
Killing and quickning, bringing down to hell
And up to heaven in an houre;
Making a chiming of a passing-bell.
We say amisse,
This or that is:
Thy word is all, if we could spell.

O that I once past changing were,
Fast in thy Paradise, where no flower can wither!
  Many a spring I shoot up fair,
Offring at heav'n, growing and groning thither:
      Nor doth my flower
      Want a spring-showre,
  My sinnes and I joining together.

  But while I grow in a straight line,
Still upwards bent, as if heav'n were mine own,
  Thy anger comes, and I decline:
What frost to that? what pole is not the zone,
      Where all things burn,
      When thou dost turn,
  And the least frown of thine is shown?

  And now in age I bud again,
After so many deaths I live and write;
  I once more smell the dew and rain,
And relish versing: O my onely light,
      It cannot be
      That I am he
  On whom thy tempests fell all night.

  These are thy wonders, Lord of love,
To make us see we are but flowers that glide:
  Which when we once can finde and prove,
Thou hast a garden for us, where to bide.
      Who would be more,
      Swelling through store,
  Forfeit their Paradise by their pride.

GEORGE HERBERT

Sonnet: Leaves

Leaves of the summer, lovely summer's pride,
   Sweet is the shade below your silent tree,
Whether in waving copses, where ye hide
   My roamings, or in fields that let me see
   The open sky; and whether ye may be
Around the low-stemm'd oak, robust and wide;
Or taper ash upon the mountain side;
   Or lowland elm; your shade is sweet to me.

Whether ye wave above the early flow'rs
   In lively green; or whether, rustling sere,
Ye fly on playful winds, around my feet,

In dying autumn; lovely are your bow'rs,
   Ye early-dying children of the year;
     Holy the silence of your calm retreat.

WILLIAM BARNES

Enid's Song

Come in, the ford is roaring on the plain,
The distant hills are pale across the rain;
Come in, come in, for open is the gate.
   Come in, poor man, and let the tempest blow.
Let Fortune frown and old possession go,
But health is wealth in high or low estate;
   Tho' Fortune frown thou shalt not hear us rail,
The frown of Fortune never turn'd us pale,
For man is man and master of his fate.
   Turn, Fortune, turn thy wheel with smile or frown,
With thy false wheel we go not up or down,
Our hoard is little but our hearts are great.
   Smile and we smile, the lords of many lands,
Frown and we smile, the lords of our own hands,
For man is man, and master of his fate.
   The river ford will fall on yonder plain,

The flying rainbow chase the flying rain,
The sun at last will smile however late;
  Come in, come in, whoever lingers there,
Nor scorn the ruin'd house and homely fare,
The house is poor but open is the gate.

ALFRED TENNYSON

The Rain that Fell upon
the Height

Your love lacks joy, your letter says.
Yes; love requires the focal space
Of recollection or of hope,
Ere it can measure its own scope.
Too soon, too soon comes Death to show
We love more deeply than we know!
The rain, that fell upon the height
Too gently to be call'd delight,
Within the dark vale reappears
As a wild cataract of tears;
And love in life should strive to see
Sometimes what love in death would be!
Easier to love, we so should find,
It is than to be just and kind.
  She's gone: shut close the coffin-lid:
What distance for another did
That death has done for her! The good,
Once gazed upon with heedless mood,
Now fills with tears the famish'd eye,
And turns all else to vanity.
'Tis sad to see, with death between,
The good we have pass'd and have not seen!
How strange appear the words of all!
The looks of those that live appal.
They are the ghosts, and check the breath:
There's no reality but death . . . .

No magic of her voice or smile
Suddenly raised a fairy isle,
But fondness for her underwent
An unregarded increment,
Like that which lifts, through centuries,
The coral-reef within the seas,
Till, lo! the land where was the wave,
Alas! 'tis everywhere her grave.

COVENTRY PATMORE

To Autumn

I

Season of mists and mellow fruitfulness,
  Close bosom-friend of the maturing sun;
Conspiring with him how to load and bless
  With fruit the vines that round the thatch-eves run;
To bend with apples the moss'd cottage-trees,
  And fill all fruit with ripeness to the core;
    To swell the gourd, and plump the hazel shells
With a sweet kernel; to set budding more,
  And still more, later flowers for the bees,
  Until they think warm days will never cease,
    For Summer has o'er-brimm'd their clammy cells.

II

Who hath not seen thee oft amid thy store?
  Sometimes whoever seeks abroad may find
Thee sitting careless on a granary floor,
  Thy hair soft-lifted by the winnowing wind;
Or on a half-reap'd furrow sound asleep,
  Drows'd with the fume of poppies, while thy hook
    Spares the next swath and all its twined flowers:
And sometimes like a gleaner thou dost keep
  Steady thy laden head across a brook;
  Or by a cyder-press, with patient look,
    Thou watchest the last oozings hours by hours.

III

Where are the songs of Spring? Ay, where are they?
   Think not of them, thou hast thy music too,—
While barred clouds bloom the soft-dying day,
   And touch the stubble-plains with rosy hue;
Then in a wailful choir the small gnats mourn
   Among the river shallows, borne aloft
      Or sinking as the light wind lives or dies;
And full-grown lambs loud bleat from hilly bourn;
   Hedge-crickets sing; and now with treble soft
The red-breast whistles from a garden-croft;
   And gathering swallows twitter in the skies.

JOHN KEATS

Now Came Still Evening On

                        Uriel to his charge
Returnd on that bright beam, whose point now rais'd
Bore him slope downward to the Sun now fall'n
Beneath th' *Azores*; whither the prime Orb,
Incredible how swift, had thither rowl'd
Diurnal, or this less volubil Earth
By shorter flight to th' East, had left him there
Arraying with reflected Purple and Gold
The Clouds that on his Western Throne attend:
Now came still Eevning on, and Twilight gray
Had in her sober Liverie all things clad;
Silence accompanied, for Beast and Bird,
They to thir grassie Couch, these to thir Nests
Were slunk, all but the wakeful Nightingale;
She all night long her amorous descant sung;
Silence was pleas'd: now glow'd the Firmament
With living Saphirs: *Hesperus* that led
The starrie Host, rode brightest, till the Moon
Rising in clouded Majestie, at length
Apparent Queen unvaild her peerless light,
And o're the dark her Silver Mantle threw.

JOHN MILTON

Calm is the Morn without a Sound

Calm is the morn without a sound,
   Calm as to suit a calmer grief,
   And only through the faded leaf
The chestnut pattering to the ground:

Calm and deep peace on this high wold,
   And on these dews that drench the furze,
   And all the silvery gossamers
That twinkle into green and gold:

Calm and still light on yon great plain
   That sweeps with all its autumn bowers,
   And crowded farms and lessening towers,
To mingle with the bounding main:

Calm and deep peace in this wide air,
   These leaves that redden to the fall;
   And in my heart, if calm at all,
If any calm, a calm despair:

Calm on the seas, and silver sleep,
   And waves that sway themselves in rest,
   And dead calm in that noble breast
Which heaves but with the heaving deep.

ALFRED TENNYSON

His Swans

Remote music of his swans, their long
Necks ahead of them, slow
Beating of their wings, in unison,
Traversing serene
Grey wide blended horizontals
Of endless sea and sky.

Their choral song: heard sadly, but not
Sad: they sing with solemnity, yet cheerfully,
Contentedly, though one by one
They die.
One by one his white birds
Falter, and fall, out of the sky.

GEOFFREY GRIGSON

Merlin's Riddling

Rain, rain, and sun! a rainbow in the sky!
A young man will be wiser by and by;
An old man's wit may wander ere he die.
Rain, rain, and sun! a rainbow on the lea!
And truth is this to me, and that to thee;
And truth or clothed or naked let it be.
Rain, sun, and rain! and the free blossom blows:
Sun, rain, and sun! and where is he who knows?
From the great deep to the great deep he goes.

ALFRED TENNYSON

O Blest Unfabled Incense Tree

O blest unfabled Incense Tree,
That burns in glorious Araby,
With red scent chalicing the air,
Till earth-life grow Elysian there!

Half buried to her flaming breast
In this bright tree, she makes her nest,
Hundred-sunned Phœnix! when she must
Crumble at length to hoary dust!

Her gorgeous death-bed! her rich pyre
Burnt up with aromatic fire!
Her urn, sight high from spoiler men!
Her birthplace when self-born again!

[65]

The mountainless green wilds among,
Here ends she her unechoing song!
With amber tears and odorous sighs
Mourned by the desert where she dies!

GEORGE DARLEY

The Music of Forefended Spheres

He that but once too nearly hears
The music of forefended spheres,
Is thenceforth lonely, and for all
His days like one who treads the Wall
Of China, and, on this hand, sees
Cities and their civilities,
And, on the other, lions.

COVENTRY PATMORE

Fair is the World

Fair is the world, now autumn's wearing,
And the sluggard sun lies long abed;
Sweet are the days, now winter's nearing,
And all winds feign that the wind is dead.

Dumb is the hedge where the crabs hang yellow,
Bright as the blossoms of the spring;
Dumb is the close where the pears grow mellow,
And none but the dauntless redbreasts sing.

Fair was the spring, but amidst his greening
Grey were the days of the hidden sun;
Fair was the summer, but overweening,
So soon his o'er-sweet days were done.

Come then, love, for peace is upon us,
Far off is failing, and far is fear,
Here where the rest in the end hath won us,
In the garnering tide of the happy year.

Come from the grey old house by the water,
Where, far from the lips of the hungry sea,
Green groweth the grass o'er the field of the slaughter,
And all is a tale for thee and me.

WILLIAM MORRIS

A Proper Sonnet, how Time Consumeth All Earthly Things

Ay me, ay me, I sigh to see the scythe afield,
Down goeth the grass, soon wrought to withered hay.
Ay me, alas! ay me, alas, that beauty needs must yield,
And princes pass, as grass doth fade away.

Ay me, ay me, that life cannot have lasting leave,
Nor gold take hold of everlasting joy.
Ay me, alas! ay me, alas, that time hath talents to receive,
And yet no time can make a sure stay.

Ay me, ay me, that wit cannot have wishèd choice,
Nor wish can win that will desires to see.
Ay me, alas! ay me, alas, that mirth can promise no rejoice,
Nor study tell what afterward shall be.

Ay me, ay me, that no sure staff is given to age,
Nor age can give sure wit that youth will take.
Ay me, alas! ay me, alas, that no counsel wise and sage
Will shun the show that all doth mar and make.

Ay me, ay me, come time, shear on and shake thy hay,
It is no boot to balk thy bitter blows.
Ay me, alas! ay me, alas, come time, take every thing away,
For all is thine, be it good or bad that grows.

THOMAS PROCTOR

Elegy
Written in a Country Church-yard

The Curfew tolls the knell of parting day,
The lowing herd wind slowly o'er the lea,
The plowman homeward plods his weary way,
And leaves the world to darkness and to me.

Now fades the glimmering landscape on the sight,
And all the air a solemn stillness holds,
Save where the beetle wheels his droning flight,
And drowsy tinklings lull the distant folds;

Save that from yonder ivy-mantled tow'r
The mopeing owl does to the moon complain
Of such, as wand'ring near her secret bow'r,
Molest her ancient solitary reign.

Beneath those rugged elms, that yew-tree's shade,
Where heaves the turf in many a mould'ring heap,
Each in his narrow cell for ever laid,
The rude Forefathers of the hamlet sleep.

The breezy call of incense-breathing Morn,
The swallow twitt'ring from the straw-built shed,
The cock's shrill clarion, or the echoing horn,
No more shall rouse them from their lowly bed.

For them no more the blazing hearth shall burn,
Or busy housewife ply her evening care:
No children run to lisp their sire's return,
Or climb his knees the envied kiss to share.

Oft did the harvest to their sickle yield,
Their furrow oft the stubborn glebe has broke;
How jocund did they drive their team afield!
How bow'd the woods beneath their sturdy stroke!

Let not Ambition mock their useful toil,
Their homely joys, and destiny obscure;
Nor Grandeur hear with a disdainful smile,
The short and simple annals of the poor.

The boast of heraldry, the pomp of pow'r,
And all that beauty, all that wealth e'er gave,
Awaits alike th' inevitable hour.
The paths of glory lead but to the grave.

Nor you, ye Proud, impute to These the fault,
If Mem'ry o'er their Tomb no Trophies raise,
Where thro' the long-drawn isle and fretted vault
The pealing anthem swells the note of praise.

Can storied urn or animated bust
Back to its mansion call the fleeting breath?
Can Honour's voice provoke the silent dust,
Or Flatt'ry sooth the dull cold ear of Death?

Perhaps in this neglected spot is laid
Some heart once pregnant with celestial fire;
Hands, that the rod of empire might have sway'd,
Or wak'd to extasy the living lyre.

But Knowledge to their eyes her ample page
Rich with the spoils of time did ne'er unroll:
Chill Penury repress'd their noble rage,
And froze the genial current of the soul.

Full many a gem of purest ray serene,
The dark unfathom'd caves of ocean bear:
Full many a flower is born to blush unseen,
And waste its sweetness on the desert air.

Some village-Hampden, that the dauntless breast
The little Tyrant of his fields withstood;
Some mute inglorious Milton here may rest,
Some Cromwell guiltless of his country's blood

Th' applause of list'ning senates to command,
The threats of pain and ruin to despise,
To scatter plenty o'er a smiling land,
And read their hist'ry in a nation's eyes,

Their lot forbad: nor circumscrib'd alone
Their growing virtues, but their crimes confin'd;
Forbad to wade through slaughter to a throne,
And shut the gates of mercy on mankind,

The struggling pangs of conscious truth to hide,
To quench the blushes of ingenuous shame,
Or heap the shrine of Luxury and Pride
With incense kindled at the Muse's flame.

Far from the madding crowd's ignoble strife,
Their sober wishes never learn'd to stray;
Along the cool sequester'd vale of life
They kept the noiseless tenor of their way.

Yet ev'n these bones from insult to protect
Some frail memorial still erected nigh,
With uncouth rhimes and shapeless sculpture deck'd,
Implores the passing tribute of a sigh.

Their name, their years, spelt by th' unletter'd muse,
The place of fame and elegy supply:
And many a holy text around she strews,
That teach the rustic moralist to die.

For who to dumb Forgetfulness a prey,
This pleasing anxious being e'er resign'd,
Left the warm precincts of the chearful day,
Nor cast one longing ling'ring look behind?

On some fond breast the parting soul relies,
Some pious drops the closing eye requires;
Ev'n from the tomb the voice of Nature cries,
Ev'n in our Ashes live their wonted Fires.

For thee, who mindful of th' unhonour'd Dead
Dost in these lines their artless tale relate;
If chance, by lonely contemplation led,
Some kindred Spirit shall inquire thy fate,

Haply some hoary-headed Swain may say,
"Oft have we seen him at the peep of dawn
"Brushing with hasty steps the dews away
"To meet the sun upon the upland lawn.

"There at the foot of yonder nodding beech
"That wreathes its old fantastic roots so high,
"His listless length at noontide would he stretch,
"And pore upon the brook that babbles by.

"Hard by yon wood, now smiling as in scorn,
"Mutt'ring his wayward fancies he would rove,
"Now drooping, woeful wan, like one forlorn,
"Or craz'd with care, or cross'd in hopeless love.

"One morn I miss'd him on the custom'd hill,
"Along the heath and near his fav'rite tree;
"Another came; nor yet beside the rill,
"Nor up the lawn, nor at the wood was he;

"The next with dirges due in sad array
"Slow thro' the church-way path we saw him born.
"Approach and read (for thou can'st read) the lay,
"Grav'd on the stone beneath yon aged thorn."

The Epitaph

Here rests his head upon the lap of Earth
A Youth to Fortune and to Fame unknown.
Fair Science frown'd not on his humble birth.
And Melancholy mark'd him for her own.

Large was his bounty, and his soul sincere,
Heav'n did a recompence as largely send:
He gave to Mis'ry all he had, a tear,
He gain'd from Heav'n ('twas all he wish'd) a friend.

No farther seek his merits to disclose,
Or draw his frailties from their dread abode,
(There they alike in trembling hope repose,)
The bosom of his Father and his God.

THOMAS GRAY

Fall, Leaves, Fall

Fall, leaves, fall; die, flowers, away;
Lengthen night and shorten day;
Every leaf speaks bliss to me
Fluttering from the autumn tree.
I shall smile when wreaths of snow
Blossom where the rose should grow;
I shall sing when night's decay
Ushers in a drearier day.

EMILY BRONTË

If Birth Persists

He sees the gentle stir of birth
When morning purifies the earth;
He leans upon a gate and sees
The pastures, and the quiet trees.
Low, woody hill, with gracious bound,
Folds the still valley almost round;
The cuckoo, loud on some high lawn,
Is answered from the depth of dawn;
In the hedge straggling to the stream,
Pale, dew-drenched, half-shut roses gleam;
But, where the farther side slopes down,
He sees the drowsy new-waked clown
In his white quaint-embroidered frock
Make, whistling, tow'rd his mist-wreathed flock—
Sowly, behind his heavy tread,
The wet, flowered grass heaves up its head.

Leaned on his gate, he gazes—tears
Are in his eyes, and in his ears
The murmur of a thousand years.
Before him he sees life unroll,
A placid and continuous whole—
That general life, which does not cease,
Whose secret is not joy, but peace;
That life, whose dumb wish is not missed
If birth proceeds, if things subsist;
The life of plants, and stones, and rain,
The life he craves—if not in vain
Fate gave, what chance shall not control,
His sad lucidity of soul.

MATTHEW ARNOLD

A Summer Night
to Geoffrey Hoyland

Out on the lawn I lie in bed,
Vega conspicuous overhead
   In the windless nights of June,
As congregated leaves complete
Their day's activity; my feet
   Point to the rising moon.

Lucky, this point in time and space
Is chosen as my working-place,
   Where the sexy airs of summer,
The bathing hours and the bare arms,
The leisured drives through a land of farms
   Are good to a newcomer.

Equal with colleagues in a ring
I sit on each calm evening
   Enchanted as the flowers
The opening light draws out of hiding
With all its gradual dove-like pleading,
   Its logic and its powers:

That later we, though parted then,
May still recall these evenings when
    Fear gave his watch no look;
The lion griefs loped from the shade
And on our knees their muzzles laid,
    And Death put down his book.

Now north and south and east and west
Those I love lie down to rest;
    The moon looks on them all,
The healers and the brilliant talkers
The eccentrics and the silent walkers,
    The dumpy and the tall.

She climbs the European sky,
Churches and power-stations lie
    Alike among earth's fixtures:
Into the galleries she peers
And blankly as a butcher stares
    Upon the marvellous pictures.

To gravity attentive, she
Can notice nothing here, though we
    Whom hunger does not move,
From gardens where we feel secure
Look up and with a sigh endure
    The tyrannies of love:

And, gentle, do not care to know,
Where Poland draws her eastern bow,
    What violence is done,
Nor ask what doubtful act allows
Our freedom in this English house,
    Our picnics in the sun.

Soon, soon, through dykes of our content
The crumpling flood will force a rent
    And, taller than a tree,
Hold sudden death before our eyes
Whose river dreams long hid the size
    And vigours of the sea.

[74]

But when the waters make retreat
And through the black mud first the wheat
   In shy green stalks appears,
When stranded monsters gasping lie,
And sounds of riveting terrify
   Their whorled unsubtle ears,

May these delights we dread to lose,
This privacy, need no excuse
   But to that strength belong,
As through a child's rash happy cries
The drowned parental voices rise
   In unlamenting song.

After discharges of alarm
All unpredicted let them calm
   The pulse of nervous nations,
Forgive the murderer in his glass,
Tough in their patience to surpass
   The tigress her swift motions.

W. H. AUDEN

Hendecasyllabics

In the month of the long decline of roses
I, beholding the summer dead before me,
Set my face to the sea and journeyed silent,
Gazing eagerly where above the sea-mark
Flame as fierce as the fervid eyes of lions
Half divided the eyelids of the sunset;
Till I heard as it were a noise of waters
Moving tremulous under feet of angels
Multitudinous, out of all the heavens;
Knew the fluttering wind, the fluttered foliage,
Shaken fitfully, full of sound and shadow;
And saw, trodden upon by noiseless angels,
Long mysterious reaches fed with moonlight,
Sweet sad straits in a soft subsiding channel,

[75]

Blown about by the lips of winds I knew not,
Winds not born in the north nor any quarter,
Winds not warm with the south nor any sunshine;
Heard between them a voice of exultation,
"Lo, the summer is dead, the sun is faded,
Even like as a leaf the year is withered,
All the fruits of the day from all her branches
Gathered, neither is any left to gather.
All the flowers are dead, the tender blossoms,
All are taken away; the season wasted,
Like an ember among the fallen ashes.
Now with light of the winter days, with moonlight,
Light of snow, and the bitter light of hoarfrost,
We bring flowers that fade not after autumn,
Pale white chaplets and crowns of latter seasons,
Fair false leaves (but the summer leaves were falser),
Woven under the eyes of stars and planets
When low light was upon the windy reaches
Where the flower of foam was blown, a lily
Dropt among the sonorous fruitless furrows
And green fields of the sea that make no pasture:
Since the winter begins, the weeping winter,
All whose flowers are tears, and round his temples
Iron blossom of frost is bound for ever."

ALGERNON CHARLES SWINBURNE

The First-Born Star

The evening comes, the fields are still.
The tinkle of the thirsty rill,
Unheard all day, ascends again;
Deserted is the half-mown plain,
Silent the swaths! the ringing wain,
The mower's cry, the dog's alarms,
All housed within the sleeping farms!
The business of the day is done,
The last-left haymaker is gone,
And from the thyme upon the height,

And from the elder-blossom white
And pale dog-roses in the hedge,
And from the mint-plant in the sedge,
In puffs of balm the night-air blows
The perfume which the day forgoes.
And on the pure horizon far,
See, pulsing with the first-born star,
The liquid sky above the hill!
The evening comes, the fields are still.

MATTHEW ARNOLD

Tristram's Song

Ay, ay, O ay—the winds that bend the brier!
A star in heaven, a star within the mere!
Ay, ay, O ay—a star was my desire,
And one was far apart, and one was near:
Ay, ay, O ay—the winds that bow the grass!
And one was water and one star was fire,
And one will ever shine and one will pass.
Ay, ay, O ay—the winds that move the mere.

ALFRED TENNYSON

The Golden Journey to Samarkand

Prologue

I

We who with songs beguile your pilgrimage
  And swear that Beauty lives though lilies die,
We Poets of the proud old lineage
  Who sing to find your hearts, we know not why,—

What shall we tell you? Tales, marvellous tales
  Of ships and stars and isles where good men rest,
Where nevermore the rose of sunset pales,
  And winds and shadows fall toward the West:

And there the world's first huge white-bearded kings
  In dim glades sleeping, murmur in their sleep,
And closer round their breasts the ivy clings,
  Cutting its pathway slow and red and deep.

II

And how beguile you? Death has no repose
  Warmer and deeper than that Orient sand
Which hides the beauty and bright faith of those
  Who made the Golden Journey to Samarkand.

And now they wait and whiten peaceably,
  Those conquerors, those poets, those so fair:
They know time comes, not only you and I,
  But the whole world shall whiten, here or there;

When those long caravans that cross the plain
  With dauntless feet and sound of silver bells
Put forth no more for glory or for gain,
  Take no more solace from the palm-girt wells.

When the great markets by the sea shut fast
  All that calm Sunday that goes on and on:
When even lovers find their peace at last,
  And Earth is but a star, that once had shone.

Epilogue
At the Gate of the Sun, Bagdad, in olden time

THE MERCHANTS (*together*)
Away, for we are ready to a man!
  Our camels sniff the evening and are glad.
Lead on, O Master of the Caravan:
  Lead on the Merchant-Princes of Bagdad.

THE CHIEF DRAPER
Have we not Indian carpets dark as wine,
  Turbans and sashes, gowns and bows and veils,
And broideries of intricate design,
  And printed hangings in enormous bales?

THE CHIEF GROCER
We have rose-candy, we have spikenard,
   Mastic and terebinth and oil and spice,
And such sweet jams meticulously jarred
   As God's own Prophet eats in Paradise.

THE PRINCIPAL JEWS
And we have manuscripts in peacock styles
   By Ali of Damascus; we have swords
Engraved with storks and apes and crocodiles,
   And heavy beaten necklaces, for Lords.

THE MASTER OF THE CARAVAN
But you are nothing but a lot of Jews.

THE PRINCIPAL JEWS
Sir, even dogs have daylight, and we pay.

THE MASTER OF THE CARAVAN
But who are ye in rags and rotten shoes,
   You dirty-bearded, blocking up the way?

THE PILGRIMS
We are the Pilgrims, master; we shall go
   Always a little further: it may be
Beyond that last blue mountain barred with snow,
   Across that angry or that glimmering sea,

White on a throne or guarded in a cave
   There lives a prophet who can understand
Why men were born: but surely we are brave,
   Who make the Golden Journey to Samarkand.

THE CHIEF MERCHANT
We gnaw the nail of hurry. Master, away!

ONE OF THE WOMEN
O turn your eyes to where your children stand.
Is not Bagdad the beautiful? O stay!

THE MERCHANTS (*in chorus*)
We take the Golden Road to Samarkand.

AN OLD MAN
Have you not girls and garlands in your homes,
  Eunuchs and Syrian boys at your command?
Seek not excess: God hateth him who roams!

THE MERCHANTS (*in chorus*)
We make the Golden Journey to Samarkand.

A PILGRIM WITH A BEAUTIFUL VOICE
Sweet to ride forth at evening from the wells
  When shadows pass gigantic on the sand,
And softly through the silence beat the bells
  Along the Golden Road to Samarkand.

A MERCHANT
We travel not for trafficking alone:
  By hotter winds our fiery hearts are fanned:
For lust of knowing what should not be known
  We make the Golden Journey to Samarkand.

THE MASTER OF THE CARAVAN
Open the gate, O watchman of the night!

THE WATCHMAN
  Ho, travellers, I open. For what land
Leave you the dim-moon city of delight?

THE MERCHANTS (*with a shout*)
We make the Golden Journey to Samarkand.

(*The Caravan passes through the gate.*)

THE WATCHMAN (*consoling the women*)
What would ye, ladies? It was ever thus.
  Men are unwise and curiously planned.

A WOMAN
They have their dreams, and do not think of us.

[80]

Siren Chorus

Troop home to silent grots and caves,
　　Troop home! and mimic as you go
The mournful winding of the waves
　　Which to their dark abysses flow.

At this sweet hour all things beside
　　In amorous pairs to covert creep,
The swans that brush the evening tide
　　Homeward in snowy couples keep.

In his green den the murmuring seal
　　Close by his sleek companion lies,
While singly we to bedward steal,
　　And close in fruitless sleep our eyes.

In bowers of love men take their rest,
　　In loveless bowers we sigh alone,
With bosom-friends are others blest,
　　But we have none! but we have none!

GEORGE DARLEY

Winter

　I, singularly moved
To love the lovely that are not beloved,
Of all the Seasons, most
Love Winter, and to trace
The sense of the Trophonian pallor on her face.
It is not death, but plenitude of peace;
And the dim cloud that does the world enfold
Hath less the characters of dark and cold

[81]

Than warmth and light asleep,
And correspondent breathing seems to keep
With the infant harvest, breathing soft below
Its eider coverlet of snow.
Nor is in field or garden anything
But, duly look'd into, contains serene
The substance of things hoped for, in the Spring,
And evidence of Summer not yet seen.
On every chance-mild day
That visits the moist shaw,
The honeysuckle, 'sdaining to be crost
In urgence of sweet life by sleet or frost,
'Voids the time's law
With still increase
Of leaflet new, and little, wandering spray;
Often, in sheltering brakes,
As one from rest disturb'd in the first hour,
Primrose or violet bewilder'd wakes,
And deems 'tis time to flower;
Though not a whisper of her voice he hear,
The buried bulb does know
The signals of the year,
And hails far Summer with his lifted spear;
The gorse-field dark, by sudden, gold caprice,
Turns, here and there, into a Jason's fleece;
Lilies, that soon in Autumn slipp'd their gowns of green
And vanish'd into earth,
And came again, ere Autumn died, to birth,
Stand full-array'd amidst the wavering shower,
And perfect for the Summer, less the flower;
In nook of pale or crevice of crude bark,
Thou canst not miss,
If close thou spy, to mark
The ghostly chrysalis,
That, if thou touch it, stirs in its dream dark;
And the flush'd Robin, in the evenings hoar,
Does of Love's Day, as if he saw it, sing;
But sweeter yet than dream or song of Summer or Spring
Are Winter's sometime smiles, that seem to well
From infancy ineffable;

Her wandering, languorous gaze,
So unfamiliar, so without amaze,
On the elemental, chill adversity,
The uncomprehended rudeness; and her sigh
And solemn, gathering tear,
And look of exile from some great repose, the sphere
Of ether, moved by ether only, or
By something still more tranquil.

COVENTRY PATMORE

The Bird of Dawning

Some say that ever 'gainst that season comes
Wherein our Saviour's birth is celebrated,
This bird of dawning singeth all night long,
And then, they say, no spirit dare stir abroad,
The nights are wholesome, then no planets strike,
No fairy takes, nor witch hath power to charm.
So hallowed and so gracious is that time.

WILLIAM SHAKESPEARE

Winter's Frosty Pangs

Come then! and while the slow icicle hangs
At the stiff thatch, and Winter's frosty pangs
Benumb the year, blithe (as of old) let us
'Midst noise and war, of peace, and mirth discuss.
This portion thou wert born for? why should we
Vex at the time's ridiculous misery?

HENRY VAUGHAN

Snow-flakes

Out of the bosom of the Air,
  Out of the cloud-folds of her garments shaken,
Over the woodlands brown and bare,
  Over the harvest-fields forsaken,
      Silent, and soft, and slow
      Descends the snow.

Even as our cloudy fancies take
  Suddenly shape in some divine expression,
Even as the troubled heart doth make
  In the white countenance confession,
      The troubled sky reveals
      The grief it feels.

This is the poem of the Air,
  Slowly in silent syllables recorded;
This is the secret of despair,
  Long in its cloudy bosom hoarded,
      Now whispered and revealed
      To wood and field.

H. W. LONGFELLOW

A Winter Night

It was a chilly winter's night;
  And frost was glitt'ring on the ground,
And evening stars were twinkling bright;
  And from the gloomy plain around
      Came no sound,
But where, within the wood-girt tow'r,
The churchbell slowly struck the hour;

As if that all of human birth
    Had risen to the final day,
And soaring from the wornout earth
    Were called in hurry and dismay,
        Far away;
And I alone of all mankind
Were left in loneliness behind.

WILLIAM BARNES

The Silent Icicles

All seasons shall be sweet to thee,
Whether the summer clothe the general earth
With greenness, or the redbreast sit and sing
Betwixt the tufts of snow on the bare branch
Of mossy apple-tree, while the nigh thatch
Smokes in the sun-thaw; whether the eave-drops fall
Heard only in the trances of the blast,
Or if the secret ministry of frost
Shall hang them up in silent icicles
Quietly shining to the quiet Moon.

SAMUEL TAYLOR COLERIDGE

Winter Evening

Over the wintry fields the snow drifts; falling, falling;
    Its frozen burden filling each hollow. And hark;
    Out of the naked woods a wild bird calling,
        On the starless verge of the dark!

WALTER DE LA MARE

Frost on the Flower

Death lies on her like an untimely frost
Upon the sweetest flower of all the field.

WILLIAM SHAKESPEARE

Of Mans First Disobedience

Of Mans First Disobedience, and the Fruit
Of that Forbidden Tree, whose mortal tast
Brought Death into the World, and all our woe,
With loss of *Eden*, till one greater Man
Restore us, and regain the blissful Seat,
Sing Heav'nly Muse, that on the secret top
Of *Oreb*, or of·*Sinai*, didst inspire
That Shepherd, who first taught the chosen Seed.
In the Beginning how the Heav'ns and Earth
Rose out of *Chaos*: or if *Sion* Hill
Delight thee more, and *Siloa*'s Brook that flow'd
Fast by the Oracle of God; I thence
Invoke thy aid to my adventrous Song,
That with no middle flight intends to soar
Above th' *Aonian* Mount, while it pursues
Things unattempted yet in Prose or Rhime.
And chiefly Thou O Spirit, that dost prefer
Before all Temples th' upright heart and pure,
Instruct me, for Thou know'st; Thou from the first
Wast present, and with mighty wings outspread
Dove-like satst brooding on the vast Abyss
And mad'st it pregnant: What in me is dark
Illumine, what is low raise and support;
That to the highth of this great Argument
I may assert Eternal Providence,
And justifie the wayes of God to men.

JOHN MILTON

The Exit from Eden

So spake our Mother *Eve*, and *Adam* heard
Well pleas'd, but answer'd not; for now too nigh
Th' Archangel stood, and from the other Hill
To thir fixt Station, all in bright array
The Cherubim descended; on the ground
Gliding meteorous, as Ev'ning Mist

Ris'n from a River o're the marish glides,
And gathers ground fast at the Labourers heel
Homeward returning. High in Front advanc't,
The brandisht Sword of God before them blaz'd
Fierce as a Comet; which with torrid heat,
And vapour as the *Libyan* Air adust,
Began to parch that temperate Clime; whereat
In either hand the hastning Angel caught
Our lingring Parents, and to th' Eastern Gate
Led them direct, and down the Cliff as fast
To the subjected Plaine; then disappeer'd.
They looking back, all th' Eastern side beheld
Of Paradise, so late thir happie seat,
Wav'd over by that flaming Brand, the Gate
With dreadful Faces throng'd and fierie Armes:
Som natural tears they drop'd, but wip'd them soon;
The World was all before them, where to choose
Thir place of rest, and Providence thir guide:
They hand in hand with wandring steps and slow,
Through *Eden* took thir solitarie way.

JOHN MILTON

The Lonely Cloud of Care

. . . do not chafe at social rules.
Leave that to charlatans and fools.
Clay graffs and clods conceive the rose,
So base still fathers best. Life owes
Itself to bread; enough thereof
And easy days condition love;
And, kindly train'd, love's roses thrive,
No more pale, scentless petals five,
Which moisten the considerate eye
To see what haste they make to die,
But heavens of colour and perfume,
Which, month by month, renew the bloom
Of art-born graces, when the year
In all the natural grove is sere.

Blame nought then! Bright let be the air
About my lonely cloud of care.

COVENTRY PATMORE

The Old Familiar Faces

Where are they gone, the old familiar faces?

I had a mother, but she died, and left me,
Died prematurely in a day of horrors—
All, all are gone, the old familiar faces.

I have had playmates, I have had companions,
In my days of childhood, in my joyful school-days—
All, all are gone, the old familiar faces.

I have been laughing, I have been carousing,
Drinking late, sitting late, with my bosom cronies—
All, all are gone, the old familiar faces.

I loved a love once, fairest among women.
Closed are her doors on me, I must not see her—
All, all are gone, the old familiar faces.

I have a friend, a kinder friend has no man.
Like an ingrate, I left my friend abruptly;
Left him, to muse on the old familiar faces.

Ghost-like, I paced round the haunts of my childhood.
Earth seem'd a desert I was bound to traverse,
Seeking to find the old familiar faces.

Friend of my bosom, thou more than a brother!
Why wert not thou born in my father's dwelling?
So might we talk of the old familiar faces.

For some they have died, and some they have left me,
And some are taken from me; all are departed;
All, all are gone, the old familiar faces.

CHARLES LAMB

L'Isolement

Souvent sur la montagne, à l'ombre du vieux chêne,
Au coucher du soleil, tristement je m'assieds;
Je promène au hasard mes regards sur la plaine,
Dont le tableau changeant se déroule à mes pieds.

Ici gronde le fleuve aux vagues écumantes;
Il serpente, et s'enfonce en un lointain obscur;
Là le lac immobile étend ses eaux dormantes
Où l'étoile du soir se lève dans l'azur.

Au sommet de ces monts couronnés de bois sombres,
Le crépuscule encor jette un dernier rayon;
Et le char vaporeux de la reine des ombres
Monte, et blanchit déjà les bords de l'horizon.

Cependant, s'élançant de la flèche gothique,
Un son religieux se répand dans les airs:
Le voyageur s'arrête, et la cloche rustique
Aux derniers bruits du jour mêle de saints concerts.

Mais à ces doux tableaux mon âme indifférente
N'éprouve devant eux ni charme ni transports;
Je contemple la terre ainsi qu'une ombre errante:
Le soleil des vivants n'échauffe plus les morts.

De colline en colline en vain portant ma vue,
Du sud à l'aquilon, de l'aurore au couchant,
Je parcours tous les points de l'immense étendue,
Et je dis: "Nulle part le bonheur ne m'attend."

Que me font ces vallons, ces palais, ces chaumières,
Vains objets dont pour moi le charme est envolé?
Fleuves, rochers, forêts, solitudes si chères,
Un seul être vous manque, et tout est dépeuplé!

Que le tour du soleil ou commence ou s'achève,
D'un œil indifférent je le suis dans son cours;
En un ciel sombre ou pur qu'il se couche ou se lève,
Qu'importe le soleil? Je n'attends rien des jours.

Quand je pourrais le suivre en sa vaste carrière,
Mes yeux verraient partout le vide et les déserts:
Je ne désire rien de tout ce qu'il éclaire;
Je ne demande rien à l'immense univers.

Mais peut-être au-delà des bornes de sa sphère,
Lieux où le vrai soleil éclaire d'autres cieux,
Si je pouvais laisser ma dépouille à la terre,
Ce que j'ai tant rêvé paraîtrait à mes yeux!

Là, je m'enivrerais à la source où j'aspire;
Là, je retrouverais et l'espoir et l'amour,
Et ce bien idéal que toute âme désire,
Et qui n'a pas de nom au terrestre séjour!

Que ne puis-je, porté sur le char de l'Aurore,
Vague objet de mes vœux, m'élancer jusqu'à toi!
Sur la terre d'exil pourquoi resté-je encore?
Il n'est rien de commun entre la terre et moi.

Quand la feuille des bois tombe dans la prairie,
Le vent du soir s'élève et l'arrache aux vallons;
Et moi, je suis semblable à la feuille flétrie:
Emportez-moi comme elle, orageux aquilons.

ALPHONSE DE LAMARTINE

The Poplar Field

The poplars are fell'd; farewell to the shade,
And the whispering sound of the cool colonnade!
The winds play no longer and sing in the leaves,
Nor Ouse on his bosom their image receives.

Twelve years have elapsed since I first took a view
Of my favourite field, and the bank where they grew;
And now in the grass behold they are laid,
And the tree is my seat that once lent me a shade!

The blackbird has fled to another retreat,
Where the hazels afford him a screen from the heat,
And the scene where his melody charm'd me before
Resounds with his sweet flowing ditty no more.

My fugitive years are all hasting away,
And I must ere long lie as lowly as they,
With a turf on my breast, and a stone at my head,
Ere another such grove shall rise in its stead.

'Tis a sight to engage me, if any thing can,
To muse on the perishing pleasures of man;
Though his life be a dream, his enjoyments, I see,
Have a being less durable even than he.

WILLIAM COWPER

The Shrubbery
Written in a Time of Affliction

Oh happy shades! to me unblest,
    Friendly to peace, but not to me,
How ill the scene that offers rest,
    And heart that cannot rest, agree!

This glassy stream, that spreading pine,
 Those alders quiv'ring to the breeze,
Might sooth a soul less hurt than mine,
 And please, if any thing could please.

But fixt unalterable care
 Foregoes not what she feels within,
Shows the same sadness ev'ry where,
 And slights the season and the scene.

For all that pleas'd in wood or lawn,
 While peace possess'd these silent bow'rs,
Her animating smile withdrawn,
 Has lost its beauties and its pow'rs.

The saint or moralist should tread
 This moss-grown alley, musing slow,
They seek like me the secret shade,
 But not like me, to nourish woe.

Me fruitful scenes and prospects waste,
 Alike admonish not to roam,
These tell me of enjoyments past,
 And those of sorrows yet to come.

WILLIAM COWPER

No Time for Lamentation Now

Come, come, no time for lamentation now,
Nor much more cause, *Samson* hath quit himself
Like *Samson*, and heroicly hath finish'd
A life Heroic, on his Enemies
Fully reveng'd, hath left them years of mourning,
And lamentation to the Sons of *Caphtor*
Through all *Philistian* bounds. To *Israel*
Honour hath left, and freedom, let but them
Find courage to lay hold on this occasion,
To himself and Fathers house eternal fame;
And which is best and happiest yet, all this
With God not parted from him, as was feard,

[92]

But favouring and assisting to the end.
Nothing is here for tears, nothing to wail
Or knock the breast, no weakness, no contempt,
Dispraise, or blame, nothing but well and fair,
And what may quiet us in a death so noble.
Let us go find the body where it lies
Sok't in his enemies blood, and from the stream
With lavers pure and cleansing herbs wash off
The clotted gore. I with what speed the while
(*Gaza* is not in plight to say us nay)
Will send for all my kindred, all my friends
To fetch him hence and solemnly attend
With silent obsequie and funeral train
Home to his Fathers house: there will I build him
A Monument, and plant it round with shade
Of Laurel ever green, and branching Palm,
With all his Trophies hung, and Acts enroll'd
In copious Legend, or sweet Lyric Song.
Thither shall all the valiant youth resort,
And from his memory inflame thir breasts
To matchless valour, and adventures high:
The Virgins also shall on feastful days
Visit his Tomb with flowers, only bewailing
His lot unfortunate in nuptial choice,
From whence captivity and loss of eyes.
  CHOR: All is best, though we oft doubt,
What th' unsearchable dispose
Of highest wisdom brings about,
And ever best found in the close.
Oft he seems to hide his face,
But unexpectedly returns
And to his faithful Champion hath in place
Bore witness gloriously; whence *Gaza* mourns
And all that band them to resist
His uncontroulable intent,
His servants he with new acquist
Of true experience from this great event
With peace and consolation hath dismist,
And calm of mind all passion spent.

JOHN MILTON

Where Lies the Land

Where lies the land to which the ship would go?
Far, far ahead, is all her seamen know.
And where the land she travels from? Away,
Far, far behind, is all that they can say.

On sunny noons upon the deck's smooth face,
Linked arm in arm, how pleasant here to pace;
Or, o'er the stern reclining, watch below
The foaming wake far widening as we go.

On stormy nights when wild north-westers rave,
How proud a thing to fight with wind and wave!
The dripping sailor on the reeling mast
Exults to bear, and scorns to wish it past.

Where lies the land to which the ship would go?
Far, far ahead, is all her seamen know.
And where the land she travels from? Away,
Far, far behind, is all that they can say.

ARTHUR HUGH CLOUGH

The Pilgrimage

I travell'd on, seeing the hill, where lay
                My expectation.
            A long it was and weary way.
            The gloomy cave of Desperation
I left on th' one, and on the other side
                The rock of Pride.

And so I came to Fancies medow strow'd
                With many a flower:
            Fain would I here have made abode,
            But I was quicken'd by my houre.
So to Cares cops I came, and there got through
                With much ado.

That led me to the wilde of Passion, which
                    Some call the wold;
            A wasted place, but sometimes rich.
            Here I was robb'd of all my gold,
Save one good Angell, which a friend had ti'd
                    Close to my side.

At length I got unto the gladsome hill,
                    Where lay my hope,
            Where lay my heart; and climbing still,
            When I had gain'd the brow and top,
A lake of brackish waters on the ground
                    Was all I found.

With that abash'd and struck with many a sting
                    Of swarming fears,
            I fell, and cry'd, Alas my King!
            Can both the way and end be tears?
Yet taking heart I rose, and then perceiv'd
                    I was deceiv'd:

My hill was further: so I flung away,
                    Yet heard a crie
            Just as I went, *None goes that way
            And lives*: If that be all, said I,
After so foul a journey death is fair,
                    And but a chair.

GEORGE HERBERT

Say not the Struggle Nought Availeth

Say not the struggle nought availeth,
  The labour and the wounds are vain,
The enemy faints not, nor faileth,
  And as things have been they remain.

If hopes were dupes, fears may be liars;
  It may be, in yon smoke concealed,
Your comrades chase e'en now the fliers,
  And, but for you, possess the field.

For while the tired waves, vainly breaking,
  Seem here no painful inch to gain,
Far back, through creeks and inlets making,
  Comes silent, flooding in, the main,

And not by eastern windows only,
  When daylight comes, comes in the light,
In front, the sun climbs slow, how slowly,
  But westward, look, the land is bright.

ARTHUR HUGH CLOUGH

A Vision

I lost the love of heaven above,
  I spurned the lust of earth below,
I felt the sweets of fancied love,
  And hell itself my only foe.

I lost earth's joys, but felt the glow
  Of heaven's flame abound in me,
Till loveliness and I did grow
  The bard of immortality.

I loved but woman fell away,
  I hid me from her faded fame,
I snatch'd the sun's eternal ray
  And wrote till earth was but a name.

In every language upon earth,
  On every shore, o'er every sea,
I gave my name immortal birth
  And kept my spirit with the free.

JOHN CLARE

Now Fades the Last Long Streak of Snow

Now fades the last long streak of snow,
   Now burgeons every maze of quick
   About the flowering squares, and thick
By ashen roots the violets blow.

Now rings the woodland loud and long,
   The distance takes a lovelier hue,
   And drowned in yonder living blue
The lark becomes a sightless song.

Now dance the lights on lawn and lea,
   The flocks are whiter down the vale,
   And milkier every milky sail
On winding stream or distant sea;

Where now the seamew pipes, or dives
   In yonder greening gleam, and fly
   The happy birds, that change their sky
To build and brood; that live their lives

From land to land; and in my breast
   Spring wakens too; and my regret
   Becomes an April violet,
And buds and blossoms like the rest.

ALFRED TENNYSON

A Robin

Ghost-grey the fall of night,
   Ice-bound the lane,
Lone in the dying light
   Flits he again;
Lurking where shadows steal,
Perched in his coat of blood,
Man's homestead at his heel,
   Death-still the wood.

[97]

Odd restless child; it's dark;
  All wings are flown
But this one wizard's—hark!
  Stone clapped on stone!
Changeling and solitary,
Secret and sharp and small,
Flits he from tree to tree,
  Calling on all.

WALTER DE LA MARE

The Robin

Poor bird! I do not envy thee;
Pleas'd in the gentle melody
  Of thine own song.
Let crabbed winter silence all
The winged choir, he never shall
  Chain up thy tongue:
    Poor innocent!
When I would please myself, I look on thee;
And guess some sparks of that felicity,
    That self-content.

When the bleak face of winter spreads
The earth, and violates the meads
  Of all their pride;
When sapless trees and flowers are fled,
Back to their causes, and lie dead
  To all beside:
    I see thee set,
Bidding defiance to the bitter air,
Upon a wither'd spray, by cold made bare,
    And drooping yet.

There, full in notes, to ravish all
My earth, I wonder what to call
    My dullness; when
I hear thee, pretty creature, bring
Thy better odes of praise, and sing,
    To puzzle men:
        Poor pious elf!
I am instructed by thy harmony,
To sing the time's uncertainty,
        Safe in my self.

Poor Redbreast, carol out thy lay,
And teach us mortals what to say.
    Here cease the choir
Of ayery choristers; no more
Mingle your notes; but catch a store
    From her sweet lyre;
        You are but weak,
Meer summer chanters; you have neither wing
Nor voice, in winter. Pretty Redbreast, sing
        What I would speak.

GEORGE DANIEL

The Time Draws Near the
Birth of Christ

The time draws near the birth of Christ:
    The moon is hid; the night is still;
    The Christmas bells from hill to hill
Answer each other in the mist.

Four voices of four hamlets round,
    From far and near, on mead and moor,
    Swell out and fail, as if a door
Were shut between me and the sound:

Each voice four changes on the wind,
    That now dilate, and now decrease,
    Peace and goodwill, goodwill and peace,
Peace and goodwill, to all mankind.

This year I slept and woke with pain,
    I almost wished no more to wake,
    And that my hold on life would break
Before I heard those bells again:

But they my troubled spirit rule,
    For they controlled me when a boy;
    They bring me sorrow touched with joy,
The merry merry bells of Yule.

ALFRED TENNYSON

Care Charming Sleep

Care charming sleep, thou easer of all woes,
Brother to death, sweetly thy self dispose
On this afflicted Prince, fall like a Cloud
In gentle showrs, give nothing that is loud,
Or painfull to his slumbers; easie, sweet,
And as a purling stream, thou son of night,
Pass by his troubled senses; sing his pain
Like hollow murmuring wind, or silver Rain,
Into this Prince gently, Oh gently slide,
And kiss him into slumbers like a Bride.

JOHN FLETCHER

To Sleep

O soft embalmer of the still midnight,
    Shutting, with careful fingers and benign,
Our gloom-pleas'd eyes, embower'd from the light,
    Enshaded in forgetfulness divine;
O soothest Sleep! if so it please thee, close,
    In midst of this thine hymn, my willing eyes,
Or wait the amen, ere thy poppy throws
    Around my bed its lulling charities;
Then save me, or the passed day will shine
Upon my pillow, breeding many woes;
    Save me from curious conscience, that still lords
Its strength for darkness, burrowing like a mole;
    Turn the key deftly in the oiled wards,
And seal the hushed casket of my soul.

JOHN KEATS

All Souls

They are chanting now the service of All the Dead
And the village folk outside in the burying-ground
Listen—except those who strive with their dead,
Reaching out in anguish, yet unable quite to touch them:
Those villagers isolated at the grave
Where the candles burn in the daylight, and the painted wreaths
Are propped on end, there, where the mystery starts.

The naked candles burn on every grave.
On your grave, in England, the weeds grow.

But I am your naked candle burning,
And that is not your grave, in England,
The world is your grave.
And my naked body standing on your grave
Upright towards heaven is burning off to you
Its flame of life, now and always, till the end.

It is my offering to you; every day is All Souls' Day.

I forget you, have forgotten you.
I am busy only at my burning,
I am busy only at my life.
But my feet are on your grave, planted.
And when I lift my face, it is a flame that goes up
To the other world, where you are now.
But I am not concerned with you.
    I have forgotten you.

I am a naked candle burning on your grave.

D. H. LAWRENCE

Giorno Dei Morti

Along the avenues of cypresses,
All in their scarlet cloaks and surplices
Of linen, go the chanting choristers,
The priests in gold and black, the villagers. . . .

And all along the path to the cemetery
The round dark heads of men crowd silently,
And black-scarved faces of womenfolk, wistfully
Watch at the banner of death, and the mystery.

And at the foot of a grave a father stands
With sunken head, and forgotten, folded hands;
And at the foot of a grave a mother kneels
With pale shut face, nor either hears nor feels

The coming of the chanting choristers
Between the avenue of cypresses,
The silence of the many villagers,
The candle-flames beside the surplices.

D. H. LAWRENCE

The Peace of a Good Mind

Why lov'st thou so this brotle worldès joy?
Take all the mirth, take all the fantasies,
Take every game, take every wanton toy,
Take every sport, that men can thee devise,
And among them all on warrantise,
Thou shalt no pleasure comparable find
To th'inward gladness of a virtuous mind.

SIR THOMAS MORE

O Gentle Sleep

How many thousand of my poorest subjects
Are at this hour asleep! O sleep, O gentle sleep,
Nature's soft nurse, how have I frighted thee,
That thou no more wilt weigh my eyelids down
And steep my senses in forgetfulness?
Why rather, sleep, liest thou in smoky cribs,
Upon uneasy pallets stretching thee
And hushed with buzzing night-flies to thy slumber,
Than in the perfumed chambers of the great,
Under the canopies of costly state,
And lulled with sound of sweetest melody?
O thou dull god, why liest thou with the vile
In loathsome beds, and leavest the kingly couch
A watch-case or a common 'larum-bell?
Wilt thou upon the high and giddy mast
Seal up the ship-boy's eyes, and rock his brains
In cradle of the rude imperious surge
And in the visitation of the winds,
Who take the ruffian billows by the top,
Curling their monstrous heads and hanging them
With deafening clamor in the slippery clouds,
That, with the hurly, death itself awakes?
Canst thou, O partial sleep, give thy repose
To the wet sea-son in an hour so rude,
And in the calmest and most stillest night,

With all appliances and means to boot,
Deny it to a king? Then happy low, lie down!
Uneasy lies the head that wears a crown.

WILLIAM SHAKESPEARE

Memento Homo quod Cinis
es et in Cinerem Reverteris

Earth out of earth is wonderly wrought,
Earth has got on earth a dignity of nought,
Earth upon earth has set all his thought,
How that earth upon earth may be high brought.

Earth upon earth would be a king,
But how that earth to earth shall, thinks he no thing.
When earth breeds earth and his rents home bring,
Then shall earth of earth have full hard parting.

Earth upon earth wins castles and towers,
Then says earth unto earth, "This is all ours."
When earth upon earth has built up his bowers
Then shall earth for earth suffer sharp scours.

Earth goes upon earth as gold upon gold,
He that goes upon earth glittering as gold,
Like as death never more go to earth should,
And yet shall earth to earth go sooner than he would.

Now why that earth loves earth, wonder methink,
Or why that earth for earth should either sweat or swink,
For when that earth upon earth is brought within brink
Then shall earth of earth have a foul stink.
Mors solvit Omnia.

ANON

O Death, Rock Me Asleep

O death, O death, rocke mee asleepe,
Bringe mee to quiett rest,
Lett passe my wearie guiltlesse Ghost
Out of my carefull brest.
    Toll on the passing bell,
    Ringe out my dolefull knell,
    Thy sound my death abroad will tell,
    For I must die:
    There is no remedie.

My paines, my paines, who can expresse?
Alas, they are so stronge,
My dolowrs will not suffer strength
My life for to prolong.
    Toll on etc.

Alone, alone in prison stronge,
I waile my destinie;
Woe worth this cruel happ, that I
Must tast this miserie.
    Toll on etc.

Farewell, farewell, my pleasures past,
Welcome my present paine:
I feele my torment so increase
That life cannot remaine.
    Cease now then, passing bell,
    Ringe out my dolefull knell,
    For thou my death doth tell;
    Lord, pittie thou my soule,
    Death doth drawe nigh;
    Sound dolefullie,
    For now I dye,
    I die, I die.

attributed to
GEORGE BOLEYN,
VISCOUNT ROCHFORD

The Garden of Proserpine

Here, where the world is quiet;
   Here, where all trouble seems
Dead winds' and spent waves' riot
   In doubtful dreams of dreams;
I watch the green field growing
For reaping folk and sowing,
For harvest-time and mowing,
   A sleepy world of streams.

I am tired of tears and laughter,
   And men that laugh and weep;
Of what may come hereafter
   For men that sow to reap:
I am weary of days and hours,
Blown buds of barren flowers,
Desires and dreams and powers
   And everything but sleep.

Here life has death for neighbour,
   And far from eye or ear
Wan waves and wet winds labour,
   Weak ships and spirits steer;
They drive adrift, and whither
They wot not who make thither;
But no such winds blow hither,
   And no such things grow here.

No growth of moor or coppice,
   No heather-flower or vine,
But bloomless buds of poppies,
   Green grapes of Proserpine,
Pale beds of blowing rushes
Where no leaf blooms or blushes
Save this whereout she crushes
   For dead men deadly wine.

Pale, without name or number,
    In fruitless fields of corn,
They bow themselves and slumber
    All night till light is born;
And like a soul belated,
In hell and heaven unmated,
By cloud and mist abated
    Comes out of darkness morn.

Though one were strong as seven,
    He too with death shall dwell,
Nor wake with wings in heaven,
    Nor weep for pains in hell;
Though one were fair as roses,
His beauty clouds and closes;
And well though love reposes,
    In the end it is not well.

Pale, beyond porch and portal,
    Crowned with calm leaves, she stands
Who gathers all things mortal
    With cold immortal hands;
Her languid lips are sweeter
Than love's who fears to greet her
To men that mix and meet her
    From many times and lands.

She waits for each and other,
    She waits for all men born;
Forgets the earth her mother,
    The life of fruits and corn;
And spring and seed and swallow
Take wing for her and follow
Where summer song rings hollow
    And flowers are put to scorn.

There go the loves that wither,
    The old loves with wearier wings;
And all dead years draw thither,
    And all disastrous things;
Dead dreams of days forsaken,
Blind buds that snows have shaken,
Wild leaves that winds have taken,
    Red strays of ruined springs.

We are not sure of sorrow,
    And joy was never sure;
To-day will die to-morrow;
    Time stoops to no man's lure;
And love, grown faint and fretful,
With lips but half regretful
Sighs, and with eyes forgetful
    Weeps that no loves endure.

From too much love of living,
    From hope and fear set free,
We thank with brief thanksgiving
    Whatever gods may be
That no life lives for ever;
That dead men rise up never;
That even the weariest river
    Winds somewhere safe to sea.

Then star nor sun shall waken,
    Nor any change of light:
Nor sound of waters shaken,
    Nor any sound or sight:
Nor wintry leaves nor vernal,
Nor days nor things diurnal;
Only the sleep eternal
    In an eternal night.

ALGERNON CHARLES SWINBURNE

Time

Unfathomable Sea! whose waves are years,
   Ocean of Time, whose waters of deep woe
Are brackish with the salt of human tears!
   Thou shoreless flood, which in thy ebb and flow
Claspest the limits of mortality,
And sick of prey, yet howling on for more,
Vomitest thy wrecks on its inhospitable shore;
Treacherous in calm, and terrible in storm,
   Who shall put forth on thee,
   Unfathomable Sea?

PERCY BYSSHE SHELLEY

Vertue

Sweet day, so cool, so calm, so bright,
The bridall of the earth and skie:
The dew shall weep thy fall to night;
      For thou must die.

Sweet rose, whose hue angrie and brave
Bids the rash gazer wipe his eye:
Thy root is ever in its grave,
      And thou must die.

Sweet spring, full of sweet dayes and roses,
A box where sweets compacted lie;
My musick shows ye have your closes,
      And all must die.

Onely a sweet and vertuous soul,
Like season'd timber, never gives;
But though the whole world turn to coal,
      Then chiefly lives.

GEORGE HERBERT

The Lyke-Wake Dirge

This ean night, this ean night,
   Every night and awle,
Fire and fleet and candle-light,
   And Christ receive thy sawle.

When thou from hence doest pass away,
   Every night and awle,
To Whinny-moor thou comest at last,
   And Christ receive thy sawle.

If ever thou gave either hosen or shoon,
   Every night and awle,
Sit thee down and put them on,
   And Christ receive thy sawle.

But if hosen or shoon thou never gave nean,
   Every night and awle,
The whinnes shall prick thee to the bare beane,
   And Christ receive thy sawle.

From Whinny-moor that thou mayst pass,
   Every night and awle,
To Brig o' Dread thou comest at last,
   And Christ receive thy sawle.

From Brig of Dread that thou mayest pass
   Every night and awle,
To Purgatory fire thou com's at last,
   And Christ receive thy sawle.

If ever thou gave either milke or drinke,
   Every night and awle,
The fire shall never make thee shrink,
   And Christ receive thy sawle.

But if milk nor drink thou never gave nean,
   Every night and awle,
The fire shall burn thee to the bare bene,
   And Christ receive thy sawle.

This ean night, this ean night,
   Every night and awle,
Fire and fleet and candle-light,
   And Christ receive thy sawle.

ANON

Immortal Longings

Give me my robe, put on my crown, I have
Immortal longings in me. Now no more
The juice of Egypt's grape shall moist this lip.
Yare, yare, good Iras; quick. Methinks I hear
Antony call: I see him rouse himself
To praise my noble act. I hear him mock
The luck of Caesar, which the gods give men
To excuse their after wrath. Husband, I come:
Now to that name my courage prove my title!
I am fire, and air; my other elements
I give to baser life. So, have you done?
Come then, and take the last warmth of my lips.
Farewell, kind Charmian, Iras, long farewell.
(*Kisses them. Iras falls and dies.*)
Have I the aspic in my lips? Dost fall?
If thou and nature can so gently part,
The stroke of death is as a lover's pinch,
Which hurts, and is desired. Dost thou lie still?

WILLIAM SHAKESPEARE

Barthram's Dirge

They shot him on the Nine-Stane Rig,
  Beside the Headless Cross;
And they left him lying in his blood,
  Upon the muir and moss.

They made a bier of the broken bough,
  The saugh and the aspen grey;
And they bore him to the Lady Chapel,
  And waked him there all day.

A lady came to that lonely bower,
  And threw her robes aside,
She tore her ling-long yellow hair,
  And knelt at Barthram's side.

She bathed him in the Lady-Well,
  His wounds sae deep and sair;
And she plaited a garland for his breast,
  And a garland for his hair.

They row'd him in a lily sheet,
And bare him to his earth,
And the Grey Friars sung the dead man's mass,
  As they pass'd the Chapel-Garth.

They buried him at the mirk midnight,
  When the dew fell cold and still,
When the aspen grey forgot to play,
  And the mist clung to the hill.

They dug his grave but a bare foot deep,
  By the edge of the Nine-Stane Burn,
And they cover'd him o'er wi' the heather-flower,
  The moss and the lady-fern.

A Grey Friar stay'd upon the grave,
　　And sang till the morning-tide;
And a friar shall sing for Barthram's soul,
　　While the Headless Cross shall bide.

ANON

If You Had Known

　　　　If you had known
When listening with her to the far-down moan
Of the white-selvaged and empurpled sea,
And rain came on that did not hinder talk,
Or damp your flashing facile gaiety
In turning home, despite the slow wet walk
By crooked ways, and over stiles of stone;
　　　　If you had known

　　　　You would lay roses,
Fifty years thence, on her monument, that discloses
Its graying shape upon the luxuriant green;
Fifty years thence to an hour, by chance led there,
What might have moved you?—yea, had you foreseen
That on the tomb of the selfsame one, gone where
The dawn of every day is as the close is,
　　　　You would lay roses!

THOMAS HARDY

Our News is Seldom Good

Our news is seldom good: the heart,
As Zola said, must always start
The day by swallowing its toad
Of failure and disgust. Our road
Gets worse and we seem altogether
Lost as our theories, like the weather,
Veer round completely every day,
And all that we can always say

[113]

Is: true democracy begins
With free confession of our sins.
In this alone are all the same,
All are so weak that none dare claim
"I have the right to govern," or
"Behold in me the Moral Law,"
And all real unity commences
In consciousness of differences,
That all have wants to satisfy
And each a power to supply.
We need to love all since we are
Each a unique particular
That is no giant, god, or dwarf,
But one odd human isomorph;
We can love each because we know
All, all of us, that this is so:
Can live since we are lived, the powers
That we create with are not ours.

O Unicorn among the cedars,
To whom no magic charm can lead us,
White childhood moving like a sigh
Through the green woods unharmed in thy
Sophisticated innocence,
To call thy true love to the dance,
O Dove of science and of light,
Upon the branches of the night,
O Ichthus playful in the deep
Sea-lodges that forever keep
Their secret of excitement hidden,
O sudden Wind that blows unbidden,
Parting the quiet reeds, O Voice
Within the labyrinth of choice
Only the passive listener hears,
O Clock and Keeper of the years,
O Source of equity and rest,
Quando non fuerit, non est,
It without image, paradigm
Of matter, motion, number, time,
The grinning gap of Hell, the hill

[114]

Of Venus and the stairs of Will,
Disturb our negligence and chill,
Convict our pride of its offence
In all things, even penitence,
Instruct us in the civil art
Of making from the muddled heart
A desert and a city where
The thoughts that have to labour there
May find locality and peace,
And pent-up feelings their release,
Send strength sufficient for our day,
And point our knowledge on its way,
O da quod jubes, Domine.

W. H. AUDEN

Apologia pro Poemate Meo

I, too, saw God through mud—
    The mud that cracked on cheeks when wretches smiled.
    War brought more glory to their eyes than blood,
    And gave their laughs more glee than shakes a child.

Merry it was to laugh there—
    Where death becomes absurd and life absurder.
    For power was on us as we slashed bones bare
    Not to feel sickness or remorse of murder.

I, too, have dropped off fear—
    Behind the barrage, dead as my platoon,
    And sailed my spirit surging light and clear
    Past the entanglement where hopes lay strewn;

And witnessed exultation—
    Faces that used to curse me, scowl for scowl,
    Shine and lift up with passion of oblation,
    Seraphic for an hour; though they were foul.

I have made fellowships—
　　Untold of happy lovers in old song.
　　For love is not the binding of fair lips
　　With the soft silk of eyes that look and long,

By Joy, whose ribbon slips—
　　But wound with war's hard wire whose stakes are strong;
　　Bound with the bandage of the arm that drips;
　　Knit in the webbing of the rifle-thong.

I have perceived much beauty
　　In the hoarse oaths that kept our courage straight;
　　Heard music in the silentness of duty;
　　Found peace where shell-storms spouted reddest spate.

Nevertheless, except you share
　　With them in hell the sorrowful dark of hell,
　　Whose world is but the trembling of a flare,
　　And heaven but as the highway for a shell,

You shall not hear their mirth:
　　You shall not come to think them well content
　　By any jest of mine. These men are worth
　　Your tears. You are not worth their merriment.

WILFRED OWEN

Thalassa

Run out the boat, my broken comrades;
Let the old seaweed crack, the surge
Burgeon oblivious of the last
Embarkation of feckless men,
Let every adverse force converge—
Here we must needs embark again.

Run up the sail, my heartsick comrades;
Let each horizon tilt and lurch—
You know the worst: your wills are fickle,
Your values blurred, your hearts impure
And your past life a ruined church—
But let your poison be your cure.

Put out to sea, ignoble comrades,
Whose record shall be noble yet;
Butting through scarps of moving marble
The narwhal dares us to be free;
By a high star our course is set,
Our end is Life. Put out to sea.

LOUIS MACNEICE

On the Death of Mr. William Hervey

Immodicis brevis est ætas, & rara Senectus. Mart.

I

It was a dismal, and a fearful night,
Scarce could the Morn drive on th'unwilling Light,
When *Sleep, Deaths Image* left my troubled brest
    By something *liker Death* possest.
My eyes with Tears did uncommanded flow,
      And on my Soul hung the dull weight
      Of some *Intolerable Fate*.
What Bell was that? Ah me! Too much I know.

II

My sweet *Companion*, and my gentle *Peere*,
Why hast thou left me thus unkindly here,
Thy *end* for ever, and my *Life* to moan;
    O thou hast left me all alone!
Thy *Soul* and *Body* when *Deaths Agonie*
      Besieg'd around thy noble heart,
      Did not with more reluctance part
Then *I*, my dearest *Friend*, do part from *Thee*.

III

My dearest *Friend*, would I had dy'd for thee!
Life and this *World* henceforth will tedious bee.
Nor shall I know hereafter what to do
      If once my *Griefs* prove *tedious* too.
Silent and sad I walk about all day,
        As sullen *Ghosts* stalk speechless by
        Where their hid *Treasures* ly;
Alas, my *Treasure*'s gone, why do I stay?

IV

He was my *Friend*, the truest *Friend* on earth;
A strong and mighty *Influence* joyn'd our *Birth*.
Nor did we envy the most sounding *Name*
      By *Friendship* giv'n of old to *Fame*.
None but his *Brethren* he, and *Sisters* knew,
        Whom the kind youth preferr'd to Me;
        And ev'n in that we did agree,
For much above my self I lov'd them too.

V

Say, for you saw us, ye immortal *Lights*,
How oft unweari'd have we spent the Nights?
Till the *Ledæan Stars* so fam'd for *Love*,
      Wondred at us from above.
We spent them not in toys, in lusts, or wine;
        But search of deep *Philosophy*,
        Wit, *Eloquence*, and *Poetry*,
Arts which I lov'd, for they, my *Friend*, were *Thine*.

VI

Ye fields of *Cambridge*, our dear *Cambridge*, say,
Have ye not seen us walking every day?
Was there a *Tree* about which did not know
      The *Love* betwixt us two?
Henceforth, ye gentle *Trees*, for ever fade;
        Or your sad branches thicker joyn,
        And into darksome shades combine,
Dark as the *Grave* wherein my *Friend* is laid.

VII

Henceforth no learned *Youths* beneath you sing,
Till all the tuneful *Birds* to your boughs they bring;
No tuneful *Birds* play with their wonted chear,
 And call the learned *Youths* to hear,
No whistling *Winds* through the glad branches fly,
 But all with sad solemnitie,
 Mute and unmoved be,
Mute as the *Grave* wherein my *Friend* does ly.

VIII

To him my *Muse* made haste with every strain
Whilst it was new, and *warm* yet from the *Brain*.
He lov'd my worthless *Rhimes*, and like a *Friend*
 Would find out something to *commend*.
Hence now, my *Muse*, thou canst not me delight;
 Be this my latest verse
 With which I now adorn his *Herse*,
And this my *Grief*, without *thy* help shall write.

IX

Had I a wreath of *Bays* about my brow,
I should contemn that flourishing honor now,
Condemn it to the *Fire*, and joy to hear
 It rage and crackle there.
Instead of *Bays*, crown with sad *Cypress* me;
 Cypress which *Tombs* does beautifie;
 Not *Phœbus* griev'd so much as I
For him, who first was made that mournful *Tree*.

X

Large was his *Soul*; as large a *Soul* as ere
Submitted to *inform* a *Body* here.
High as the Place 'twas shortly in *Heav'n* to have,
 But low, and humble as his *Grave*.
So *high* that all the *Virtues* there did come
 As to their chiefest seat
 Conspicuous, and great;
So *low* that for *Me* too it made a room.

XI

He scorn'd this busie world below, and all
That we, *Mistaken Mortals*, Pleasure call;
Was fill'd with innocent *Gallantry* and *Truth*,
       Triumphant ore the sins of *Youth*.
He like the *Stars*, to which he now is gone,
       That shine with beams like *Flame*,
       Yet burn not with the same,
Had all the *Light* of *Youth*, of the *Fire* none.

XII

Knowledge he only sought, and so soon caught,
As if for him *Knowledge* had rather *sought*.
Nor did more *Learning* every crowded lie
       In such a short *Mortalitie*.
When ere the skilful *Youth* discourst or writ,
       Still did the *Notions* throng
       About his eloquent Tongue,
Nor could his *Ink* flow faster then his *Wit*.

XIII

So strong a *Wit* did *Nature* to him frame,
As all things but his *Judgement* overcame;
His *Judgement* like the heav'nly *Moon* did show,
       Temp'ring that mighty *Sea* below.
Oh had he liv'd in *Learnings World*, what bound
       Would have been able to controul
       His over-powering Soul?
We have lost in him *Arts* that not yet are *found*.

XIV

His *Mirth* was the pure *Spirits* of various Wit,
Yet never did his *God* or *Friends* forget.
And when deep talk and wisdom came in view,
       Retir'd and gave to them their due.
For the rich help of *Books* he always took,
       Though his own searching mind before
       Was so with *Notions* written ore
As if wise *Nature* had made that her *Book*.

XV

So many *Virtues* joyn'd in him, as we
Can scarce pick here and there in *Historie*.
More then old *Writers Practice* ere could reach,
    As much as they could ever *teach*.
These did *Religion, Queen* of Virtues sway,
    And all their sacred *Motions* steare,
    Just like the First and *Highest Sphere*
Which wheels about, and turns all *Heav'n* one way.

XVI

With as much Zeal, Devotion, Pietie,
He always *Liv'd*, as other Saints do *Dye*.
Still with his soul severe account he kept,
    Weeping all *Debts* out ere he slept.
Then down in peace and innocence he lay,
    Like the *Suns* laborious light,
    Which still in *Water* sets at Night,
Unsullied with his *Journey* of the *Day*.

XVII

Wondrous young Man, why wert thou made so good,
To be snatcht hence ere better *understood*?
Snatcht before half of thee enough was seen!
    Thou Ripe, and yet thy *Life* but *Green*!
Nor could thy Friends take their last sad Farewel,
    But Danger and *Infectious Death*
    Malitiously seiz'd on that Breath
Where *Life, Spirit, Pleasure* always us'd to dwell.

XVIII

But happy Thou, ta'ne from this frantick age,
Where *Ignorance* and *Hypocrisie* does rage!
A fitter *time* for Heav'n no soul ere chose,
    The place now onely free from those.
There 'mong the *Blest* thou dost for ever shine,
    And wheresoere thou casts thy view
    Upon that white and radiant crew,
See'st not a *Soul* cloath'd with more *Light* then *Thine*.

XIX

And if the glorious *Saints* cease not to know
Their wretched Friends who *fight* with *Life* below;
Thy Flame to *Me* does still the same abide,
    Onely more pure and rarifi'd.
There whilst immortal Hymns thou dost reherse,
    Thou dost with holy pity see
    Our dull and earthly *Poesie*,
Where *Grief* and *Misery* can be join'd with *Verse*.

ABRAHAM COWLEY

His Golden Locks Time Hath to Silver Turned

His golden locks time hath to silver turned;
  O time too swift, O swiftness never ceasing!
His youth 'gainst time and age hath ever spurned,
  But spurned in vain; youth waneth by increasing:
Beauty, strength, youth, are flowers but fading seen;
Duty, faith, love, are roots, and ever green.

His helmet now shall make a hive for bees;
  And, lovers' sonnets turned to holy psalms,
A man-at-arms must now serve on his knees,
  And feed on prayers, which are age's alms:
But though from court to cottage he depart,
His saint is sure of his unspotted heart.

And when he saddest sits in homely cell,
  He'll teach his swains this carol for a song:
"Blest be the hearts that wish my sovereign well,
  Curst be the souls that think her any wrong."
Goddess, allow this aged man his right,
To be your beadsman now, that was your knight.

GEORGE PEELE

Hesperus

Hesperus! the day is gone,
Soft falls the silent dew,
A tear is now on many a flower
And heaven lives in you.

Hesperus! the evening mild
Falls round us soft and sweet.
'Tis like the breathings of a child
When day and evening meet.

Hesperus! the closing flower
Sleeps on the dewy ground,
While dews fall in a silent shower
And heaven breathes around.

Hesperus! thy twinkling ray
Beams in the blue of heaven,
And tells the traveller on his way
That Earth shall be forgiven!

JOHN CLARE

For the Bed at Kelmscott

The wind's on the wold
And the night is a-cold,
And Thames runs chill
Twixt mead and hill,
But kind and dear
Is the old house here,
And my heart is warm
Midst winter's harm.
Rest, then and rest,
And think of the best
Twixt summer and spring
When all birds sing
In the town of the tree,

And ye lie in me
But scarce dare move
Lest earth and its love
Should fade away
Ere the full of the day.

I am old and have seen
Many things that have been,
Both grief and peace,
And wane and increase.
No tale I tell
Of ill or well,
But this I say,
Night treadeth on day,
And for worst and best
Right good is rest.

WILLIAM MORRIS

May and Death

I

I wish that when you died last May,
   Charles, there had died along with you
Three parts of spring's delightful things;
   Ay, and, for me, the fourth part too.

II

A foolish thought, and worse, perhaps!
   There must be many a pair of friends
Who, arm in arm, deserve the warm
   Moon-births and the long evening-ends.

III

So, for their sake, be May still May!
   Let their new time, as mine of old,
Do all it did for me: I bid
   Sweet sights and sounds throng manifold.

IV

Only, one little sight, one plant,
  Woods have in May, that starts up green
Save a sole streak which, so to speak,
  Is spring's blood, spilt its leaves between—

V

That, they might spare; a certain wood
  Might miss the plant; their loss were small:
But I—whene'er the leaf grows there,
  Its drop comes from my heart, that's all.

ROBERT BROWNING

Love Lives Beyond the Tomb

  Love lives beyond
The tomb, the earth, which fades like dew—
  I love the fond,
The faithful, and the true.

  Love lies in sleep,
The happiness of healthy dreams,
  Eve's dews may weep,
But love delightful seems.

  'Tis seen in flowers,
And in the even's pearly dew
  On earth's green hours,
And in the heaven's eternal blue.

  'Tis heard in spring
When light and sunbeams, warm and kind,
  On angel's wing
Bring love and music to the wind.

  And where is voice
So young, so beautiful, and sweet
  As nature's choice,
Where spring and lovers meet?

[125]

Love lives beyond
The tomb, the earth, the flowers, and dew.
  I love the fond,
The faithful, young, and true.

JOHN CLARE

The Parable of the Old Man
and the Young

So Abram rose, and clave the wood, and went,
And took the fire with him, and a knife.
And as they sojourned both of them together,
Isaac the first-born spake and said, My Father,
Behold the preparations, fire and iron,
But where the lamb for this burnt-offering?
Then Abram bound the youth with belts and straps,
And builded parapets and trenches there,
And stretchèd forth the knife to slay his son.
When lo! an angel called him out of heaven,
Saying, Lay not thy hand upon the lad,
Neither do anything to him. Behold,
A ram, caught in a thicket by its horns;
Offer the Ram of Pride instead of him.
But the old man would not so, but slew his son,
And half the seed of Europe, one by one.

WILFRED OWEN

Before Agincourt

Now entertain conjecture of a time
When creeping murmur and the poring dark
Fills the wide vessel of the universe.
From camp to camp, through the foul womb of night,
The hum of either army stilly sounds,
That the fixed sentinels almost receive
The secret whispers of each other's watch.
Fire answers fire, and through their paly flames

Each battle sees the other's umbered face.
Steed threatens steed, in high and boastful neighs
Piercing the night's dull ear; and from the tents
The armorers accomplishing the knights,
With busy hammers closing rivets up,
Give dreadful note of preparation.
The country cocks do crow, the clocks do toll
And the third hour of drowsy morning name.
Proud of their numbers and secure in soul,
The confident and over-lusty French
Do the low-rated English play at dice;
And chide the cripple tardy-gaited night
Who like a foul and ugly witch doth limp
So tediously away. The poor condemnèd English,
Like sacrifices, by their watchful fires
Sit patiently and inly ruminate
The morning's danger; and their gesture sad,
Investing lank-lean cheeks and war-worn coats,
Presenteth them unto the gazing moon
So many horrid ghosts. O, now, who will behold
The royal captain of this ruined band
Walking from watch to watch, from tent to tent,
Let him cry, "Praise and glory on his head!"
For forth he goes and visits all his host,
Bids them good morrow with a modest smile
And calls them brothers, friends, and countrymen.
Upon his royal face there is no note
How dread an army hath enrounded him;
Nor doth he dedicate one jot of color
Unto the weary and all-watchèd night,
But freshly looks, and overbears attaint
With cheerful semblance and sweet majesty;
That every wretch, pining and pale before,
Beholding him, plucks comfort from his looks.
A largess universal, like the sun.
His liberal eye doth give to every one,
Thawing cold fear, that mean and gentle all
Behold, as may unworthiness define,
A little touch of Harry in the night.

WILLIAM SHAKESPEARE

The Flowers of the Forest
Lament for Flodden

I've heard the lilting at our yowe-milking,
   Lasses a-lilting before the dawn o' day;
But now they are moaning on ilka green loaning:
   "The Flowers of the Forest are a' wede away."

At buchts, in the morning, nae blythe lads are scorning;
   The lasses are lonely, and dowie, and wae;
Nae daffin', nae gabbin', but sighing and sabbing:
   Ilk ane lifts her leglen, and hies her away.

In hairst, at the shearing, nae youths now are jeering,
   The bandsters are lyart, and runkled and grey;
At fair or at preaching, nae wooing, nae fleeching:
   The Flowers of the Forest are a' wede away.

At e'en, in the gloaming, nae swankies are roaming
   'Bout stacks wi' the lasses at bogle to play,
But ilk ane sits drearie, lamenting her dearie:
   The Flowers of the Forest are a' wede away.

Dule and wae for the order sent our lads to the Border;
   The English, for ance, by guile wan the day;
The Flowers of the Forest, that foucht aye the foremost,
   The prime o' our land, are cauld in the clay.

We'll hear nae mair lilting at our yowe-milking,
   Women and bairns are heartless and wae;
Sighing and moaning on ilka green loaning:
   "The Flowers of the Forest are a' wede away."

JANE ELLIOT

yowe: ewe
loaning: meadow
wede: withered
buchts: sheepfolds
dowie: melancholy
daffin': merriment
gabbin': joking

leglen: milk pail
hairst: harvest
bandsters: binders of sheaves
lyart: grey
fleeching: coaxing
swankies: lively youngsters

Hohenlinden

On Linden, when the sun was low,
All bloodless lay the untrodden snow,
And dark as winter was the flow
    Of Iser, rolling rapidly.

But Linden saw another sight
When the drum beat at dead of night,
Commanding fires of death to light
    The darkness of her scenery.

By torch and trumpet fast arrayed,
Each horseman drew his battle blade,
And furious every charger neighed
    To join the dreadful revelry.

Then shook the hills with thunder riven,
Then rushed the steed to battle driven,
And louder than the bolts of heaven
    Far flashed the red artillery.

But redder yet that light shall glow
On Linden's hills of stainèd snow,
And bloodier yet the torrent flow
    Of Iser, rolling rapidly.

'Tis morn, but scarce yon level sun
Can pierce the war-clouds, rolling dun,
Where furious Frank and fiery Hun
    Shout in their sulphurous canopy.

The combat deepens. On, ye brave,
Who rush to glory, or the grave!
Wave, Munich! all thy banners wave,
    And charge with all thy chivalry!

Few, few shall part where many meet!
The snow shall be their winding-sheet,
And every turf beneath their feet
    Shall be a soldier's sepulchre.

THOMAS CAMPBELL

Anthem for Doomed Youth

What passing-bells for these who die as cattle?
    Only the monstrous anger of the guns.
    Only the stuttering rifles' rapid rattle
Can patter out their hasty orisons.
No mockeries now for them; no prayers nor bells,
    Nor any voice of mourning save the choirs—
The shrill, demented choirs of wailing shells;
    And bugles calling for them from sad shires.

What candles may be held to speed them all?
    Not in the hands of boys, but in their eyes
Shall shine the holy glimmers of good-byes.
    The pallor of girls' brows shall be their pall;
Their flowers the tenderness of patient minds,
And each slow dusk a drawing-down of blinds.

WILFRED OWEN

Greater Love

Red lips are not so red
    As the stained stones kissed by the English dead.
Kindness of wooed and wooer
Seems shame to their love pure.
O Love, your eyes lose lure
    When I behold eyes blinded in my stead!

Your slender attitude
  Trembles not exquisite like limbs knife-skewed,
Rolling and rolling there
Where God seems not to care;
Till the fierce love they bear
  Cramps them in death's extreme decrepitude.

Your voice sings not so soft—
  Though even as wind murmuring through raftered loft—
Your dear voice is not dear,
Gentle, and evening clear,
As theirs whom none now hear,
  Now earth has stopped their piteous mouths that coughed.

Heart, you were never hot
  Nor large, nor full like hearts made great with shot;
And though your hand be pale,
Paler are all which trail
Your cross through flame and hail:
  Weep, you may weep, for you may touch them not.

WILFRED OWEN

The Burial of Sir John Moore
after Corunna

Not a drum was heard, not a funeral note,
  As his corse to the rampart we hurried;
Not a soldier discharged his farewell shot
  O'er the grave where our hero we buried.

We buried him darkly at dead of night,
  The sods with our bayonets turning,
By the struggling moonbeam's misty light
  And the lanthorn dimly burning.

No useless coffin enclosed his breast,
  Not in sheet or in shroud we wound him;
But he lay like a warrior taking his rest
  With his martial cloak around him.

Few and short were the prayers we said,
    And we spoke not a word of sorrow;
But we steadfastly gazed on the face that was dead,
    And we bitterly thought of the morrow.

We thought, as we hollowed his narrow bed
    And smoothed down his lonely pillow,
That the foe and the stranger would tread o'er his head,
    And we far away on the billow!

Lightly they'll talk of the spirit that's gone,
    And o'er his cold ashes upbraid him—
But little he'll reck, if they let him sleep on
    In the grave where a Briton has laid him.

But half of our heavy task was done
    When the clock struck the hour for retiring;
And we heard the distant and random gun
    That the foe was sullenly firing.

Slowly and sadly we laid him down,
    From the field of his fame fresh and gory;
We carved not a line, and we raised not a stone,
    But we left him alone with his glory.

CHARLES WOLFE

And There Was a Great Calm

On the Signing of the Armistice, Nov. 11, 1918

I

There had been years of Passion—scorching, cold,
And much Despair, and Anger heaving high,
Care whitely watching, Sorrows manifold,
Among the young, among the weak and old,
And the pensive Spirit of Pity whispered, "Why?"

II

Men had not paused to answer. Foes distraught
Pierced the thinned peoples in a brute-like blindness,
Philosophies that sages long had taught,
And Selflessness, were as an unknown thought,
And "Hell!" and "Shell!" were yapped at Lovingkindness.

III

The feeble folk at home had grown full-used
To "dug-outs", "snipers", "Huns", from the war-adept
In the mornings heard, and at evetides perused;
To day-dreamt men in millions, when they mused—
To nightmare-men in millions when they slept.

IV

Waking to wish existence timeless, null,
Sirius they watched above where armies fell;
He seemed to check his flapping when, in the lull
Of night a boom came thencewise, like the dull
Plunge of a stone dropped into some deep well.

V

So, when old hopes that earth was bettering slowly
Were dead and damned, there sounded "War is done!"
One morrow. Said the bereft, and meek, and lowly,
"Will men some day be given to grace? yea, wholly,
And in good sooth, as our dreams used to run?"

VI

Breathless they paused. Out there men raised their glance
To where had stood those poplars lank and lopped,
As they had raised it through the four years' dance
Of Death in the now familiar flats of France;
And murmured, "Strange, this! How? All firing stopped?"

VII

Aye; all was hushed. The about-to-fire fired not,
The aimed-at moved away in trance-lipped song.
One checkless regiment slung a clinching shot
And turned. The Spirit of Irony smirked out, "What?
Spoil peradventures woven of Rage and Wrong?"

VIII

Thenceforth no flying fires inflamed the gray,
No hurtlings shook the dewdrop from the thorn,
No moan perplexed the mute bird on the spray;
Worn horses mused: "We are not whipped to-day";
No weft-winged engines blurred the moon's thin horn.

IX

Calm fell. From Heaven distilled a clemency;
There was peace on earth, and silence in the sky;
Some could, some could not, shake off misery:
The Sinister Spirit sneered: "It had to be!"
And again the Spirit of Pity whispered, "Why?"

THOMAS HARDY

Strange Meeting

It seemed that out of battle I escaped
Down some profound dull tunnel, long since scooped
Through granites which titanic wars had groined.
Yet also there encumbered sleepers groaned,
Too fast in thought or death to be bestirred.
Then, as I probed them, one sprang up, and stared
With piteous recognition in fixed eyes,
Lifting distressful hands as if to bless.
And by his smile, I knew that sullen hall,
By his dead smile I knew we stood in Hell.
With a thousand pains that vision's face was grained;
Yet no blood reached there from the upper ground,
And no guns thumped, or down the flues made moan.
"Strange friend," I said, "here is no cause to mourn."

"None," said that other, "save the undone years,
The hopelessness. Whatever hope is yours,
Was my life also; I went hunting wild
After the wildest beauty in the world,
Which lies not calm in eyes, or braided hair,
But mocks the steady running of the hour,
And if it grieves, grieves richlier than here.
For of my glee might many men have laughed,
And of my weeping something had been left,
Which must die now. I mean the truth untold,
The pity of war, the pity war distilled.
Now men will go content with what we spoiled,
Or, discontent, boil bloody, and be spilled.
They will be swift with swiftness of the tigress.
None will break ranks, though nations trek from progress.
Courage was mine, and I had mystery,
Wisdom was mine, and I had mastery:
To miss the march of this retreating world
Into vain citadels that are not walled.
Then, when much blood had clogged their chariot-wheels,
I would go up and wash them from sweet wells,
Even with truths that lie too deep for taint.
I would have poured my spirit without stint
But not through wounds; not on the cess of war.
Foreheads of men have bled where no wounds were.
I am the enemy you killed, my friend.
I knew you in this dark: for so you frowned
Yesterday through me as you jabbed and killed.
I parried; but my hands were loath and cold.
Let us sleep now. . . ."

WILFRED OWEN

The End

After the blast of lightning from the east,
The flourish of loud clouds, the Chariot Throne;
After the drums of time have rolled and ceased,
And by the bronze west long retreat is blown,

Shall Life renew these bodies? Of a truth
All death will he annul, all tears assuage?—
Or fill these void veins full again with youth,
And wash, with an immortal water, Age?

When I do ask white Age he saith not so:
"My head hangs weighed with snow."
And when I hearken to the Earth, she saith:
"My fiery heart shrinks, aching. It is death.
Mine ancient scars shall not be glorified,
Nor my titanic tears, the seas, be dried."

WILFRED OWEN

That Time of Year Thou Mayst in Me Behold

That time of year thou mayst in me behold
When yellow leaves, or none, or few, do hang
Upon those boughs which shake against the cold,
Bare ruined choirs where late the sweet birds sang.
In me thou seest the twilight of such day
As after sunset fadeth in the west,
Which by and by black night doth take away,
Death's second self that seals up all in rest.
In me thou seest the glowing of such fire
That on the ashes of his youth doth lie,
As the deathbed whereon it must expire,
Consumed with that which it was nourished by.
  This thou perceiv'st, which makes thy love more strong,
  To love that well which thou must leave ere long.

WILLIAM SHAKESPEARE

Tichborne's Elegy

Written in the Tower Before His Execution, 1586

My prime of youth is but a frost of cares;
  My feast of joy is but a dish of pain;
My crop of corn is but a field of tares;
  And all my good is but vain hope of gain:
The day is past, and yet I saw no sun;
And now I live, and now my life is done.

My tale was heard, and yet it was not told;
  My fruit is fall'n, and yet my leaves are green;
My youth is spent, and yet I am not old;
  I saw the world, and yet I was not seen:
My thread is cut, and yet it is not spun;
And now I live, and now my life is done.

I sought my death, and found it in my womb;
  I looked for life, and saw it was a shade;
I trod the earth, and knew it was my tomb;
  And now I die, and now I was but made:
My glass is full, and now my glass is run;
And now I live, and now my life is done.

CHIDIOCK TICHBORNE

So All Day Long the Noise of Battle Rolled

So all day long the noise of battle rolled
Among the mountains by the winter sea;
Until King Arthur's Table, man by man,
Had fallen in Lyonnesse about their lord,
King Arthur. Then, because his wound was deep,
The bold Sir Bedivere uplifted him,
And bore him to a chapel nigh the field,
A broken chancel with a broken cross,
That stood on a dark strait of barren land:
On one side lay the Ocean, and on one
Lay a great water, and the moon was full.

ALFRED TENNYSON

But Now Farewell

"But now farewell. I am going a long way
With these thou seèst—if indeed I go
(For all my mind is clouded with a doubt)—
To the island-valley of Avilion;
Where falls not hail, or rain, or any snow,
Nor ever wind blows loudly; but it lies
Deep-meadowed, happy, fair with orchard lawns
And bowery hollows crowned with summer sea,
Where I will heal me of my grievous wound."

So said he, and the barge with oar and sail
Moved from the brink, like some full-breasted swan
That, fluting a wild carol ere her death,
Ruffles her pure cold plume, and takes the flood
With swarthy webs. Long stood Sir Bedivere
Revolving many memories, till the hull
Looked one black dot against the verge of dawn,
And on the mere the wailing died away.

But when that moan had past for evermore,
The stillness of the dead world's winter dawn
Amazed him, and he groaned, "The King is gone."
And therewithal came on him the weird rhyme,
"From the great deep to the great deep he goes."

ALFRED TENNYSON

No Longer Mourn for Me
when I am Dead

No longer mourn for me when I am dead
Than you shall hear the surly sullen bell
Give warning to the world that I am fled
From this vile world, with vilest worms to dwell.
Nay, if you read this line, remember not
The hand that writ it, for I love you so
That I in your sweet thoughts would be forgot

If thinking on me then should make you woe.
O, if, I say, you look upon this verse
When I, perhaps, compounded am with clay,
Do not so much as my poor name rehearse,
But let your love even with my life decay,
    Lest the wise world should look into your moan
    And mock you with me after I am gone.

WILLIAM SHAKESPEARE

The Tongues of Dying Men

O, but they say the tongues of dying men
Enforce attention like deep harmony.
Where words are scarce, they are seldom spent in vain,
For they breathe truth that breathe their words in pain.
He that no more must say is listened more
    Than they whom youth and ease have taught to glose.
More are men's ends marked than their lives before.
    The setting sun, and music at the close,
As the last taste of sweets, is sweetest last,
Writ in remembrance more than things long past.

WILLIAM SHAKESPEARE

Let's Talk of Graves

            Of comfort no man speak!
Let's talk of graves, of worms, and epitaphs,
Make dust our paper, and with rainy eyes
Write sorrow on the bosom of the earth.
Let's choose executors and talk of wills.
And yet not so—for what can we bequeath,
Save our deposèd bodies to the ground?
Our lands, our lives, and all are Bolingbroke's,
And nothing can we call our own but death
And that small model of the barren earth
Which serves as paste and cover to our bones.

For God's sake let us sit upon the ground
And tell sad stories of the death of kings!
How some have been deposed, some slain in war,
Some haunted by the ghosts they have deposed,
Some poisoned by their wives, some sleeping killed—
All murdered; for within the hollow crown
That rounds the mortal temples of a king
Keeps Death his court; and there the antic sits,
Scoffing his state and grinning at his pomp;
Allowing him a breath, a little scene,
To monarchize, be feared, and kill with looks;
Infusing him with self and vain conceit,
As if this flesh which walls about our life
Were brass impregnable; and humored thus,
Comes at the last, and with a little pin
Bores through his castle wall, and farewell king!

WILLIAM SHAKESPEARE

Composed upon Westminster Bridge
Sept. 3, 1802

Earth has not anything to show more fair:
Dull would he be of soul who could pass by
A sight so touching in its majesty:
This City now doth, like a garment, wear
The beauty of the morning; silent, bare,
Ships, towers, domes, theatres, and temples lie
Open unto the fields, and to the sky;
All bright and glittering in the smokeless air.
Never did sun more beautifully steep
In his first splendour, valley, rock, or hill;
Ne'er saw I, never felt, a calm so deep!
The river glideth at his own sweet will:
Dear God! the very houses seem asleep;
And all that mighty heart is lying still!

WILLIAM WORDSWORTH

In Patterdale

The mind of Man is fram'd even like the breath
And harmony of music. There is a dark
Invisible workmanship that reconciles
Discordant elements, and makes them move
In one society. Ah me! that all
The terrors, all the early miseries
Regrets, vexations, lassitudes, that all
The thoughts and feelings which have been infus'd
Into my mind, should ever have made up
The calm existence that is mine when I
Am worthy of myself! Praise to the end!
Thanks likewise for the means! But I believe
That Nature, oftentimes, when she would frame
A favor'd Being, from his earliest dawn
Of infancy doth open up the clouds,
As at the touch of lightning, seeking him
With gentlest visitation; not the less,
Though haply aiming at the self-same end,
Does it delight her sometimes to employ
Severer interventions, ministry
More palpable, and so she dealt with me.

One evening (surely I was led by her)
I went alone into a Shepherd's Boat,
A Skiff that to a Willow tree was tied
Within a rocky Cave, its usual home.
'Twas by the shores of Patterdale, a Vale
Wherein I was a Stranger, thither come
A School-boy Traveller, at the Holidays.
Forth rambled from the Village Inn alone
No sooner had I sight of this small Skiff,
Discover'd thus by unexpected chance,
Than I unloos'd her tether and embark'd.
The moon was up, the Lake was shining clear
Among the hoary mountains; from the Shore
I push'd, and struck the oars and struck again
In cadence, and my little Boat mov'd on
Even like a Man who walks with stately step

[141]

Though bent on speed. It was an act of stealth
And troubled pleasure; not without the voice
Of mountain-echoes did my Boat move on,
Leaving behind her still on either side
Small circles glittering idly in the moon,
Until they melted all into one track
Of sparkling light. A rocky Steep uprose
Above the Cavern of the Willow tree
And now, as suited one who proudly row'd
With his best skill, I fix'd a steady view
Upon the top of that same craggy ridge,
The bound of the horizon, for behind
Was nothing but the stars and the grey sky.
She was an elfin Pinnace; lustily
I dipp'd my oars into the silent Lake,
And, as I rose upon the stroke, my Boat
Went heaving through the water, like a Swan;
When from behind that craggy Steep, till then
The bound of the horizon, a huge Cliff,
As if with voluntary power instinct,
Uprear'd its head. I struck, and struck again,
And, growing still in stature, the huge Cliff
Rose up between me and the stars, and still,
With measur'd motion, like a living thing,
Strode after me. With trembling hands I turn'd,
And through the silent water stole my way
Back to the Cavern of the Willow tree.
There, in her mooring-place, I left my Bark,
And, through the meadows homeward went, with grave
And serious thoughts; and after I had seen
That spectacle, for many days, my brain
Work'd with a dim and undetermin'd sense
Of unknown modes of being; in my thoughts
There was a darkness, call it solitude,
Or blank desertion, no familiar shapes
Of hourly objects, images of trees,
Of sea or sky, no colours of green fields;
But huge and mighty Forms that do not live
Like living men mov'd slowly through the mind
By day and were the trouble of my dreams.

Wisdom and Spirit of the universe!
Thou Soul that art the eternity of thought!
That giv'st to forms and images a breath
And everlasting motion! not in vain,
By day or star-light thus from my first dawn
Of Childhood didst Thou intertwine for me
The passions that build up our human Soul,
Not with the mean and vulgar works of Man,
But with high objects, with enduring things,
With life and nature, purifying thus
The elements of feeling and of thought,
And sanctifying, by such discipline,
Both pain and fear, until we recognize
A grandeur in the beatings of the heart.

Nor was this fellowship vouchsaf'd to me
With stinted kindness. In November days,
When vapours, rolling down the valleys, made
A lonely scene more lonesome; among woods
At noon, and 'mid the calm of summer nights,
When, by the margin of the trembling Lake,
Beneath the gloomy hills I homeward went
In solitude, such intercourse was mine;
'Twas mine among the fields both day and night,
And by the waters all the summer long.

And in the frosty season, when the sun
Was set, and visible for many a mile
The cottage windows through the twilight blaz'd,
I heeded not the summons:—happy time
It was, indeed, for all of us; to me
It was a time of rapture: clear and loud
The village clock toll'd six; I wheel'd about,
Proud and exulting, like an untired horse,
That cares not for his home.—All shod with steel,
We hiss'd along the polish'd ice, in games
Confederate, imitative of the chace
And woodland pleasures, the resounding horn,
The Pack loud bellowing, and the hunted hare.
So through the darkness and the cold we flew,

And not a voice was idle; with the din,
Meanwhile, the precipices rang aloud,
The leafless trees, and every icy crag
Tinkled like iron, while the distant hills
Into the tumult sent an alien sound
Of melancholy, not unnoticed, while the stars,
Eastward, were sparkling clear, and in the west
The orange sky of evening died away.

  Not seldom from the uproar I retired
Into a silent bay, or sportively
Glanced sideway, leaving the tumultuous throng,
To cut across the image of a star
That gleam'd upon the ice: and oftentimes
When we had given our bodies to the wind,
And all the shadowy banks, on either side,
Came sweeping through the darkness, spinning still
The rapid line of motion; then at once
Have I, reclining back upon my heels,
Stopp'd short, yet still the solitary Cliffs
Wheeled by me, even as if the earth had roll'd
With visible motion her diurnal round;
Behind me did they stretch in solemn train
Feebler and feebler, and I stood and watch'd
Till all was tranquil as a dreamless sleep.

WILLIAM WORDSWORTH

Newton's Statue

  The Evangelist St John my patron was:
Three Gothic courts are his, and in the first
Was my abiding-place, a nook obscure;
Right underneath, the College kitchens made
A humming sound, less tuneable than bees,
But hardly less industrious; with shrill notes
Of sharp command and scolding intermixed.
Near me hung Trinity's loquacious clock,
Who never let the quarters, night or day,

[144]

Slip by him unproclaimed, and told the hours
Twice over with a male and female voice.
Her pealing organ was my neighbour too;
And from my pillow, looking forth by light
Of moon or favouring stars, I could behold
The antechapel where the statue stood
Of Newton with his prism and silent face,
The marble index of a mind for ever
Voyaging through strange seas of Thought, alone.

WILLIAM WORDSWORTH

Animula Vagula, Blandula

Animula vagula, blandula,
Hospes comésque corporis,
Quæ nunc abibis in loca?
Pallidula, querula, nudula,
Nec, ut soles, dabis jocos.

My soul, my pleasant soul and witty,
The guest and consort of my body,
Into what place now all alone
Naked and sad wilt thou be gone?
No mirth, no wit, as heretofore,
Nor Jests wilt thou afford me more.

HADRIAN
translated from the Latin
by Henry Vaughan

What is this Knowledge?

What is this *knowledge*? but the Skie-stolne fire,
  For which the *Thiefe* still chaind in Ice doth sit?
  And which the poore rude *Satyre* did admire,
  And needs would kisse, but burnt his lips with it?

[145]

What is it? but the cloud emptie of Raine,
  Which when *Joves* Guest embrac't, he Monsters got?
  Or the false *Pailes*, which oft being fild with paine,
  Receiv'd the water, but retain'd it not?

Shortly what is it? but the fierie *Coach*
  Which the *Youth* sought, and sought his death withall?
  Or the *Boyes* wings, which when he did approch
  The *Sunnes* hote beames, did melt and let him fall?

And yet, alas, when all our Lampes are burnd,
  Our Bodies wasted, and our Spirits spent,
  When we have all the learned *Volumes* turnd,
  Which yeeld mens wits both helpe, and ornament;

What can we know? or what can we discerne?
  When *Error* chokes the windowes of the mind;
  The diverse formes of things how can we learne,
  That have bene ever from our birth-day blind?

When *Reasons* lampe which like the *Sunne* in skie,
  Throughout *Mans* litle world her beams did spread,
  Is now become a Sparkle, which doth lie
  Under the Ashes, halfe extinct and dead:

How can we hope, that through the Eye and Eare,
  This dying Sparkle, in this cloudie place,
  Can recollect those beames of knowledge cleare,
  Which were enfus'd, in the first minds by grace?

All things without, which round about we see,
  We seeke to know, and have therewith to do:
  But that whereby we *reason, live, and be,*
  Within our selves, we strangers are theretoo.

We seeke to know the moving of each *Spheare*,
  And the straunge cause of th'ebs and flouds of *Nile*:
  But of that clocke, which in our breasts we beare,
  The subtill motions, we forget the while.

We that acquaint our selves with every *Zoane*,
    And passe both *Tropikes*, and behold both *Poles*;
    When we come home, are to our selves unknowne,
    And unacquainted still with our owne *Soules*.

We studie *Speech*; but others we perswade;
    We *Leech-craft* learne, but others Cure with it;
    We'interpret *Lawes*, which other men have made,
    But reade not those, which in our harts are writ:

I know my Bodi's of so fraile a kinde,
    As force without, feavers within can kill;
    I know the heavenly nature of my mind,
    But tis corrupted both in *wit* and *will*:

I know my *Soule* hath power to know all things,
    Yet is she blind and ignorant in all;
    I know I'am one of *Natures* litle kings,
    Yet to the least and vilest things am thrall.

I know my life's a paine, and but a span,
    I know my *Sense* is mockt with every thing;
    And to conclude, *I know* my selfe a *Man*,
    Which is a *proud* and yet a *wretched* thing.

SIR JOHN DAVIES

They Are All Gone into the World of Light

They are all gone into the world of light!
    And I alone sit lingring here;
Their very memory is fair and bright,
    And my sad thoughts doth clear.

It glows and glitters in my cloudy brest
    Like stars upon some gloomy grove,
Or those faint beams in which this hill is drest,
    After the Sun's remove.

I see them walking in an Air of glory,
    Whose light doth trample on my days:
My days, which are at best but dull and hoary,
    Meer glimering and decays.

O holy hope! and high humility,
    High as the Heavens above!
These are your walks, and you have shew'd them me
    To kindle my cold love,

Dear, beauteous death! the Jewel of the Just,
    Shining nowhere, but in the dark;
What mysteries do lie beyond thy dust;
    Could man outlook that mark!

He that hath found some fledg'd birds nest, may know
    At first sight, if the bird be flown;
But what fair Well, or Grove he sings in now,
    That is to him unknown.

And yet, as Angels in some brighter dreams
    Call to the soul, when man doth sleep:
So some strange thoughts transcend our wonted theams,
    And into glory peep.

If a star were confin'd into a Tomb
    Her captive flames must needs burn there;
But when the hand that lockt her up, gives room,
    She'l shine through all the sphære.

O Father of eternal life, and all
    Created glories under thee!
Resume thy spirit from this world of thrall
    Into true liberty.

Either disperse these mists, which blot and fill
    My perspective (still) as they pass,
Or else remove me hence unto that hill,
    Where I shall need no glass.

They are all gone into the world of light!
    And I alone sit lingring here;
Their very memory is fair and bright,
    And my sad thoughts doth clear.

HENRY VAUGHAN

Elegy on Shakespeare

Renowned Spenser lye a thought more nye
To learned Chaucer, and rare Beaumont lye
A little neerer Spenser, to make roome
For Shakespeare in your threefold, fowerfold Tombe.
To lodge all foure in one bed make a shift
Untill Doomesdaye, for hardly will a fift
Betwixt this day and that by Fate be slayne,
For whom your Curtaines may be drawn againe.
If your precedency in death doth barre
A fourth place in your sacred sepulcher,
Under this carved marble of thine owne,
Sleepe, rare Tragædian, Shakespeare, sleep alone;
Thy unmolested peace, unshared Cave,
Possesse as Lord, not Tenant, of thy Grave,
    That unto us and others it may be
    Honor hereafter to be layde by thee.

WILLIAM BASSE

Earth, Receive an Honoured Guest

Earth, receive an honoured guest:
William Yeats is laid to rest.
Let the Irish vessel lie
Emptied of its poetry.

In the nightmare of the dark
All the dogs of Europe bark,
And the living nations wait,
Each sequestered in its hate;

Intellectual disgrace
Stares from every human face,
And the seas of pity lie
Locked and frozen in each eye.

Follow, poet, follow right
To the bottom of the night,
With your unconstraining voice
Still persuade us to rejoice;

With the farming of a verse
Make a vineyard of the curse,
Sing of human unsuccess
In a rapture of distress;

In the deserts of the heart
Let the healing fountain start,
In the prison of his days
Teach the free man how to praise.

W. H. AUDEN

Sweet Suffolk Owl

Sweet Suffolk owl, so trimly dight
With feathers, like a lady bright,
Thou sing'st alone, sitting by night,
Te whit, te whoo! Te whit, te whoo!

Thy note, that forth so freely rolls,
With shrill command the mouse controls;
And sings a dirge for dying souls,
Te whit, te whoo! Te whit, te whoo!

ANON

I Have Been a Foster

I have been a foster long and many day,
  My locks ben hoar.
I shall hang up my horn by the greenwood spray.
  Foster will I be no more.

All the whiles that I may my bow bend
  Shall I wed no wife.
I shall bigg me a bower at the wood's end,
  There to lead my life.

ANON

foster: forester

from The Rubáiyát of Omar Khayyám

I

Come, fill the Cup, and in the fire of Spring
Your Winter-garment of Repentance fling:
  The Bird of Time has but a little way
To flutter—and the Bird is on the Wing.

Whether at Naishápúr or Babylon,
Whether the Cup with sweet or bitter run,
  The Wine of Life keeps oozing drop by drop,
The Leaves of Life keep falling one by one.

II

A Book of Verses underneath the Bough,
A Jug of Wine, a Loaf of Bread—and Thou
  Beside me singing in the Wilderness—
Oh, Wilderness were Paradise enow!

Some for the Glories of This World; and some
Sigh for the Prophet's Paradise to come;
    Ah, take the Cash, and let the Credit go,
Nor heed the rumble of a distant Drum!

Look to the blowing Rose about us—"Lo,
Laughing," she says, "into the world I blow,
    At once the silken tassel of my Purse
Tear, and its Treasure on the Garden throw."

And those who husbanded the Golden grain,
And those who flung it to the winds like Rain,
    Alike to no such aureate Earth are turn'd
As, buried once, Men want dug up again.

The Worldly Hope men set their Hearts upon
Turns Ashes—or it prospers; and anon,
    Like Snow upon the Desert's dusty Face,
Lighting a little hour or two—is gone.

Think, in this batter'd Caravanserai
Whose Portals are alternate Night and Day,
    How Sultán after Sultán with his Pomp
Abode his destined Hour, and went his way.

They say the Lion and the Lizard keep
The Courts where Jamshýd gloried and drank deep:
    And Bahrám, that great Hunter—the Wild Ass
Stamps o'er his Head, but cannot break his Sleep.

I sometimes think that never blows so red
The Rose as where some buried Cæsar bled;
    That every Hyacinth the Garden wears
Dropt in her Lap from some once lovely Head.

And this reviving Herb whose tender Green
Fledges the River-Lip on which we lean—
    Ah, lean upon it lightly! for who knows
From what once lovely Lip it springs unseen!

Ah, my Belovèd, fill the Cup that clears
TO-DAY of past Regrets and Future Fears:
　　To-morrow!—Why, To-morrow I may be
Myself with Yesterday's Sev'n thousand Years.

For some we loved, the loveliest and the best
That from his Vintage rolling Time hath prest,
　　Have drunk their Cup a Round or two before,
And one by one crept silently to rest.

And we, that now make merry in the Room
They left, and Summer dresses in new bloom,
　　Ourselves must we beneath the Couch of Earth
Descend—ourselves to make a Couch—for whom?

Ah, make the most of what we yet may spend,
Before we too into the Dust descend;
　　Dust into Dust, and under Dust to lie
Sans Wine, sans Song, sans Singer, and—sans End!

Alike for those who for TO-DAY prepare,
And those that after some TO-MORROW stare,
　　A Muezzín from the Tower of Darkness cries,
"Fools! your Reward is neither Here nor There."

Why, all the Saints and Sages who discuss'd
Of the Two Worlds so wisely—they are thrust
　　Like foolish Prophets forth; their Words to Scorn
Are scatter'd, and their Mouths are stopt with Dust.

Myself when young did eagerly frequent
Doctor and Saint, and heard great argument
　　About it and about: but evermore
Came out by the same door where in I went.

With them the seed of Wisdom did I sow,
And with mine own hand wrought to make it grow;
　　And this was all the Harvest that I reap'd—
"I came like Water, and like Wind I go."

Into this Universe, and *Why* not knowing
Nor *Whence*, like Water willy-nilly flowing;
   And out of it, as Wind along the Waste,
I know not *Whither*, willy-nilly blowing.

III

Oh threats of Hell and Hopes of Paradise!
One thing at least is certain—*This* Life flies;
   One thing is certain and the rest is Lies;
The Flower that once has blown for ever dies.

Strange, is it not? that of the myriads who
Before us pass'd the door of Darkness through,
   Not one returns to tell us of the Road,
Which to discover we must travel too.

The Revelations of Devout and Learn'd
Who rose before us, and as Prophets burn'd,
   Are all but Stories, which, awoke from Sleep
They told their comrades, and to Sleep return'd.

I sent my Soul through the Invisible,
Some letter of that After-life to spell:
   And by and by my Soul return'd to me,
And answer'd "I Myself am Heav'n and Hell":

Heav'n but the Vision of fulfill'd Desire,
And Hell the Shadow from a Soul on fire,
   Cast on the Darkness into which Ourselves,
So late emerged from, shall so soon expire.

We are no other than a moving row
Of Magic Shadow-shapes that come and go
   Round with the Sun-illumined Lantern held
In Midnight by the Master of the Show;

But helpless Pieces of the Game He plays
Upon this Chequer-board of Nights and Days;
   Hither and thither moves, and checks, and slays,
And one by one back in the Closet lays.

The Moving Finger writes; and, having writ,
Moves on: nor all your Piety nor Wit
   Shall lure it back to cancel half a Line,
Nor all your Tears wash out a Word of it.

And that inverted Bowl they call the Sky,
Whereunder crawling coop'd we live and die,
   Lift not your hands to *It* for help—for It
As impotently moves as you or I.

With Earth's first Clay They did the Last Man knead,
And there of the Last Harvest sow'd the Seed:
   And the first Morning of Creation wrote
What the Last Dawn of Reckoning shall read.

YESTERDAY *This* Day's Madness did prepare;
TO-MORROW's Silence, Triumph, or Despair:
   Drink! for you know not whence you came, nor why:
Drink! for you know not why you go, nor where.

EDWARD FITZGERALD

Booz Endormi

Booz s'était couché de fatigue accablé;
Il avait tout le jour travaillé dans son aire;
Puis avait fait son lit à sa place ordinaire;
Booz dormait auprès des boisseaux pleins de blé.

Ce vieillard possédait des champs de blés et d'orge;
Il était, quoique riche, à la justice enclin;
Il n'avait pas de fange en l'eau de son moulin;
Il n'avait pas d'enfer dans le feu de sa forge.

Sa barbe était d'argent comme un ruisseau d'avril.
Sa gerbe n'était point avare ni haineuse;
Quand il voyait passer quelque pauvre glaneuse:
"Laissez tomber exprès des épis," disait-il.

Cet homme marchait pur loin des sentiers obliques,
Vêtu de probité candide et de lin blanc;
Et, toujours du côté des pauvres ruisselant,
Ses sacs de grains semblaient des fontaines publiques.

Booz était bon maître et fidèle parent;
Il était généreux, quoiqu'il fût économe;
Les femmes regardaient Booz plus qu'un jeune homme,
Car le jeune homme est beau, mais le vieillard est grand.

Le vieillard, qui revient vers la source première,
Entre aux jours éternels et sort des jours changeants;
Et l'on voit de la flamme aux yeux des jeunes gens,
Mais dans l'œil du vieillard on voit de la lumière.

Donc, Booz dans la nuit dormait parmi les siens.
Près des meules, qu'on eût prises pour des décombres,
Les moissonneurs couchés faisaient des groupes sombres;
Et ceci se passait dans des temps très anciens.

Les tribus d'Israël avaient pour chef un juge;
La terre, où l'homme errait sous la tente, inquiet
Des empreintes de pieds de géants qu'il voyait,
Était mouillée encor et molle du déluge.

Comme dormait Jacob, comme dormait Judith,
Booz, les yeux fermés, gisait sous la feuillée;
Or, la porte du ciel s'étant entre-bâillée
Au-dessus de sa tête, un songe en descendit.

Et ce songe était tel, que Booz vit un chêne
Qui, sorti de son ventre, allait jusqu'au ciel bleu;
Une race y montait comme une longue chaîne;
Un roi chantait en bas, en haut mourait un Dieu.

Et Booz murmurait avec la voix de l'âme:
"Comment se pourrait-il que de moi ceci vînt?
Le chiffre de mes ans a passé quatre-vingt,
Et je n'ai pas de fils, et je n'ai plus de femme.

"Voilà longtemps que celle avec qui j'ai dormi,
O Seigneur! a quitté ma couche pour la vôtre;
Et nous sommes encor tout mêlés l'un à l'autre,
Elle à demi vivante et moi mort à demi.

"Une race naîtrait de moi! Comment le croire?
Comment se pourrait-il que j'eusse des enfants?
Quand on est jeune, on a des matins triomphants;
Le jour sort de la nuit comme d'une victoire;

"Mais, vieux, on tremble ainsi qu'à l'hiver le bouleau;
Je suis veuf, je suis seul, et sur moi le soir tombe,
Et je courbe, ô mon Dieu! mon âme vers la tombe,
Comme un bœuf ayant soif penche son front vers l'eau."

Ainsi parlait Booz dans le rêve et l'extase,
Tournant vers Dieu ses yeux par le sommeil noyés;
Le cèdre ne sent pas une rose à sa base,
Et lui ne sentait pas une femme à ses pieds.

VICTOR HUGO

Death Be not Proud

Death be not proud, though some have called thee
Mighty and dreadfull, for, thou art not soe,
For, those, whom thou think'st, thou dost overthrow,
Die not, poore death, nor yet canst thou kill mee.
From rest and sleepe, which but thy pictures bee,
Much pleasure, then from thee, much more must flow,
And soonest our best men with thee doe goe,
Rest of their bones, and soules deliverie.
Thou art slave to Fate, Chance, kings, and desperate men,
And dost with poyson, warre, and sickness dwell,
And poppie, or charmes can make us sleepe as well,
And better then thy stroake; why swell'st thou then?
One short sleepe past, wee wake eternally,
And death shall be no more; death, thou shalt die.

JOHN DONNE

Sound the Trumpet, Beat the Drum

MARS: Sound the Trumpet, Beat the Drum,
        Through all the World around;
        Sound a Reveille, Sound, Sound,
           The Warrior God is come.

CHO. OF ALL: *Sound the Trumpet*, &c.

MOMUS: Thy Sword within the Scabbard keep,
          And let Mankind agree;
        Better the World were fast asleep,
          Than kept awake by Thee.
        The Fools are only thinner,
          With all our Cost and Care;
        But neither side a winner,
          For Things are as they were.

CHO. OF ALL: *The Fools are only*, &c.
        (*Enter* VENUS.)

VENUS: Calms appear, when Storms are past;
        Love will have his Hour at last:
        Nature is my kindly Care;
        Mars destroys, and I repair;
        Take me, take me, while you may,
        Venus comes not ev'ry Day.

CHO. OF ALL: *Take her, take her*, &c.

CHRONOS: The World was then so light,
        I scarcely felt the Weight;
        Joy rul'd the Day, and Love the Night.
        But since the Queen of Pleasure left the Ground,
          I faint, I lag,
           And feebly drag
        The pond'rous Orb around.

MOMUS: All, all, of a piece throughout;
        (*Pointing to* DIANA)
        Thy Chase had a Beast in View;
        (*To* MARS)
        Thy Wars brought nothing about;
        (*To* VENUS)
        Thy Lovers were all untrue.

JANUS: 'Tis well an Old Age is out,

[158]

CHRONOS: And time to begin a New.
CHO. OF ALL: *All, all, of a piece throughout;*
            Thy Chase had a Beast in View;
            Thy Wars brought nothing about;
            Thy Lovers were all untrue.
            'Tis well an Old Age is out,
            And time to begin a New.

JOHN DRYDEN

To-Morrow and To-Morrow
and To-Morrow

She should have died hereafter:
There would have been a time for such a word.
To-morrow, and to-morrow, and to-morrow
Creeps in this petty pace from day to day
To the last syllable of recorded time,
And all our yesterdays have lighted fools
The way to dusty death. Out, out, brief candle!
Life's but a walking shadow, a poor player
That struts and frets his hour upon the stage
And then is heard no more. It is a tale
Told by an idiot, full of sound and fury,
Signifying nothing.

WILLIAM SHAKESPEARE

A Winged Heart

Sickness and death, you are but sluggish things,
And cannot reach, a heart that hath got wings.

HENRY VAUGHAN

Extempore Effusion upon the Death of
James Hogg

When first, descending from the moorlands,
I saw the Stream of Yarrow glide
Along a bare and open valley,
The Ettrick Shepherd was my guide.

When last along its banks I wandered,
Through groves that had begun to shed
Their golden leaves upon the pathways,
My steps the Border-minstrel led.

The mighty Minstrel breathes no longer,
'Mid mouldering ruins low he lies;
And death upon the braes of Yarrow,
Has closed the Shepherd-poet's eyes:

Nor has the rolling year twice measured,
From sign to sign, its steadfast course,
Since every mortal power of Coleridge
Was frozen at its marvellous source;

The rapt One, of the godlike forehead,
The heaven-eyed creature sleeps in earth:
And Lamb, the frolic and the gentle,
Has vanished from his lonely hearth.

Like clouds that rake the mountain-summits,
Or waves that own no curbing hand,
How fast has brother followed brother
From sunshine to the sunless land!

Yet I, whose lids from infant slumber
Were earlier raised, remain to hear
A timid voice, that asks in whispers,
"Who next will drop and disappear?"

Our haughty life is crowned with darkness,
Like London with its own black wreath,
On which with thee, O Crabbe! forth-looking,
I gazed from Hampstead's breezy heath.

As if but yesterday departed,
Thou too art gone before; but why,
O'er ripe fruit, seasonably gathered,
Should frail survivors heave a sigh?

Mourn rather for that holy Spirit,
Sweet as the spring, as ocean deep;
For Her who, ere her summer faded,
Has sunk into a breathless sleep.

No more of old romantic sorrows,
For slaughtered Youth or love-lorn Maid!
With sharper grief is Yarrow smitten,
And Ettrick mourns with her their Poet dead.

WILLIAM WORDSWORTH

The Wild Swans at Coole

The trees are in their autumn beauty,
The woodland paths are dry,
Under the October twilight the water
Mirrors a still sky;
Upon the brimming water among the stones
Are nine-and-fifty swans.

The nineteenth autumn has come upon me
Since I first made my count;
I saw, before I had well finished,
All suddenly mount
And scatter wheeling in great broken rings
Upon their clamorous wings.

I have looked upon those brilliant creatures,
And now my heart is sore.
All's changed since I, hearing at twilight,
The first time on this shore,
The bell-beat of their wings above my head,
Trod with a lighter tread.

Unwearied still, lover by lover,
They paddle in the cold
Companionable streams or climb the air;
Their hearts have not grown old;
Passion or conquest, wander where they will,
Attend upon them still.

But now they drift on the still water,
Mysterious, beautiful;
Among what rushes will they build,
By what lake's edge or pool
Delight men's eyes when I awake some day
To find they have flown away?

W. B. YEATS

It is a Beauteous Evening, Calm and Free

It is a beauteous evening, calm and free,
The holy time is quiet as a Nun
Breathless with adoration; the broad sun
Is sinking down in its tranquillity;
The gentleness of heaven broods o'er the Sea:
Listen! the mighty Being is awake,
And doth with his eternal motion make
A sound like thunder—everlastingly.
Dear Child! dear Girl! that walkest with me here,
If thou appear untouched by solemn thought,
Thy nature is not therefore less divine:
Thou liest in Abraham's bosom all the year;
And worship'st at the Temple's inner shrine,
God being with thee when we know it not.

WILLIAM WORDSWORTH

The Owl

Downhill I came, hungry, and yet not starved;
Cold, yet had heat within me that was proof
Against the North wind; tired, yet so that rest
Had seemed the sweetest thing under a roof.

Then at the inn I had food, fire, and rest,
Knowing how hungry, cold, and tired was I.
All of the night was quite barred out except
An owl's cry, a most melancholy cry

Shaken out long and clear upon the hill,
No merry note, nor cause of merriment,
But one telling me plain what I escaped
And others could not, that night, as in I went.

And salted was my food, and my repose,
Salted and sobered, too, by the bird's voice
Speaking for all who lay under the stars,
Soldiers and poor, unable to rejoice.

EDWARD THOMAS

Up-hill

Does the road wind up-hill all the way?
   Yes, to the very end.
Will the day's journey take the whole long day?
   From morn to night, my friend.

But is there for the night a resting-place?
   A roof for when the slow dark hours begin.
May not the darkness hide it from my face?
   You cannot miss that inn.

Shall I meet other wayfarers at night?
  Those who have gone before.
Then must I knock, or call when just in sight?
  They will not keep you standing at that door.

Shall I find comfort, travel-sore and weak?
  Of labour you shall find the sum.
Will there be beds for me and all who seek?
  Yea, beds for all who come.

CHRISTINA ROSSETTI

Vitae Summa Brevis Spem nos Vetat Incohare Longam

They are not long, the weeping and the laughter,
  Love and desire and hate:
I think they have no portion in us after
    We pass the gate.

They are not long, the days of wine and roses:
  Out of a misty dream
Our path emerges for a while, then closes
    Within a dream.

ERNEST DOWSON

Stances

Tircis, il faut penser à faire la retraite;
La course de nos jours est plus qu'à demi faite;
L'âge insensiblement nous conduit à la mort:
Nous avons assez vu sur la mer de ce monde
Errer au gré des flots notre nef vagabonde;
Il est temps de jouir des délices du port.

Le bien de la fortune est un bien périssable;
Quand on bâtit sur elle, on bâtit sur le sable;
Plus on est élevé, plus on court de dangers;
Les grands pins sont en butte aux coups de la tempête,
Et la rage des vents brise plutôt le faîte
Des maisons de nos rois que les toits des bergers.

O bienheureux celui qui peut de sa mémoire
Effacer pour jamais ce vain espoir de gloire,
Dont l'inutile soin traverse nos plaisirs;
Et qui, loin retiré de la foule importune,
Vivant dans sa maison, content de sa fortune,
A, selon son pouvoir, mesuré ses désirs!

Il laboure le champ que labourait son père;
Il ne s'informe point de ce qu'on délibère
Dans ces graves conseils d'affaires accablés;
Il voit sans intérêt la mer grosse d'orages,
Et n'observe des vents les sinistres présages,
Que pour le soin qu'il a du salut de ses blés.

Roi de ses passions, il a ce qu'il désire.
Son fertile domaine est son petit empire,
Sa cabane est son Louvre et son Fontainebleau;
Ses champs et ses jardins sont autant de provinces,
Et sans porter envie à la pompe des princes
Se contente chez lui de les voir en tableau.

Il voit de toutes parts combler d'heur sa famille,
La javelle à plein poing tomber sous sa faucille,
Le vendangeur ployer sous le faix des paniers;
Et semble qu'à l'envi les fertiles montagnes,
Les humides vallons, et les grasses campagnes
S'efforcent à remplir sa cave et ses greniers.

Il suit aucune fois un cerf par les foulées,
Dans ces vieilles forêts du peuple reculées,
Et qui même du jour ignorent le flambeau;
Aucune fois des chiens il suit les voix confuses,
Et voit enfin le lièvre, après toutes ses ruses,
Du lieu de sa naissance en faire son tombeau.

Tantôt il se promène au long de ses fontaines,
De qui les petits flots font luire dans les plaines
L'argent de leurs ruisseaux parmi l'or des moissons;
Tantôt il se repose, avecque les bergères,
Sur des lits naturels de mousse et de fougères,
Qui n'ont d'autres rideaux que l'ombre des buissons.

Il soupire en repos l'ennui de sa vieillesse,
Dans ce même foyer où sa tendre jeunesse
A vu dans le berceau ses bras emmaillotés;
Il tient par les moissons registre des années,
Et voit de temps en temps leurs courses enchaînées
Vieillir avecque lui les bois qu'il a plantés.

Il ne va point fouiller aux terres inconnues,
A la merci des vents et des ondes chenues,
Ce que nature avare a caché de trésors;
Et ne recherche point, pour honorer sa vie
De plus illustre mort, ni plus digne d'envie,
Que de mourir au lit où ses pères sont morts.

Il contemple, du port, les insolentes rages
Des vents de la faveur, auteurs de nos orages,
Allumer des mutins les desseins factieux;
Et voit en un clin d'œil, par un contraire échange,
L'un déchiré du peuple au milieu de la fange
Et l'autre à même temps élevé dans les cieux.

S'il ne possède point ces maisons magnifiques,
Ces tours, ces chapiteaux, ces superbes portiques
Où la magnificence étale ses attraits,
Il jouit des beautés qu'ont les saisons nouvelles;
Il voit de la verdure et des fleurs naturelles,
Qu'en ces riches lambris l'on ne voit qu'en portraits.

Crois-moi, retirons-nous hors de la multitude,
Et vivons désormais loin de la servitude
De ces palais dorés où tout le monde accourt:
Sous un chêne élevé les arbrisseaux s'ennuient,
Et devant le soleil tous les astres s'enfuient,
De peur d'être obligés de lui faire la cour.

Après qu'on a suivi sans aucune assurance
Cette vaine faveur qui nous paît d'espérance,
L'envie en un moment tous nos desseins détruit;
Ce n'est qu'une fumée; il n'est rien de si frêle;
Sa plus belle moisson est sujette à la grêle,
Et souvent elle n'a que des fleurs pour du fruit.

Agréables déserts, séjour de l'innocence,
Où loin des vanités, de la magnificence,
Commence mon repos et finit mon tourment,
Vallons, fleuves, rochers, plaisante solitude,
Si vous fûtes témoins de mon inquiétude,
Soyez-le désormais de mon contentement!

HONORAT DE RACAN

Behold the Child

Behold the child, by Nature's kindly law,
Pleas'd with a rattle, tickled with a straw:
Some livelier play-thing gives his youth delight,
A little louder, but as empty quite:
Scarfs, garters, gold, amuse his riper stage;
And beads and pray'r-books are the toys of age:
Pleas'd with this bauble still, as that before;
'Till tir'd he sleeps, and Life's poor play is o'er. . . .

ALEXANDER POPE

There Was a Boy

There was a Boy; ye knew him well, ye cliffs
And islands of Winander!—many a time,
At evening, when the earliest stars began
To move along the edges of the hills,
Rising or setting, would he stand alone,
Beneath the trees, or by the glimmering lake;
And there, with fingers interwoven, both hands
Pressed closely palm to palm and to his mouth
Uplifted, he, as through an instrument,
Blew mimic hootings to the silent owls,
That they might answer him.—And they would shout
Across the watery vale, and shout again,
Responsive to his call—with quivering peals,
And long halloos, and screams, and echoes loud
Redoubled and redoubled; concourse wild
Of jocund din! And, when there came a pause
Of silence such as baffled his best skill:
Then, sometimes, in that silence, while he hung
Listening, a gentle shock of mild surprise
Has carried far into his heart the voice
Of mountain-torrents; or the visible scene
Would enter unawares into his mind
With all its solemn imagery, its rocks,
Its woods, and that uncertain heaven received
Into the bosom of the steady lake.

This boy was taken from his mates, and died
In childhood, ere he was full twelve years old.
Pre-eminent in beauty is the vale
Where he was born and bred: the churchyard hangs
Upon a slope above the village-school;
And, through that churchyard when my way has led
On summer-evenings, I believe, that there
A long half-hour together I have stood
Mute—looking at the grave in which he lies!

WILLIAM WORDSWORTH

The Sunbeam Said, Be Happy

Bleak season was it, turbulent and bleak,
When hitherward we journeyed, side by side,
Through bursts of sunshine and through flying showers,
Paced the long Vales, how long they were, and yet
How fast that length of way was left behind,
   Wensley's rich Vale and Sedbergh's naked heights.
The frosty wind, as if to make amends
For its keen breath, was aiding to our steps,
And drove us onward like two ships at sea,
Or like two Birds, companions in mid air,
Parted and re-united by the blast.
Stern was the face of Nature; we rejoiced
In that stern countenance, for our Souls thence drew
A feeling of their strength. The naked Trees,
The icy brooks, as on we passed, appeared
To question us. "Whence come ye? to what end?"
They seemed to say; "What would ye," said the shower,
"Wild Wanderers, whither through my dark domain?"
The sunbeam said, "be happy". When this Vale
We entered, bright and solemn was the sky
That faced us with a passionate welcoming,
And led us to our threshold.

WILLIAM WORDSWORTH

A Ship, an Isle, a Sickle Moon

A ship, an isle, a sickle moon—
With few but with how splendid stars
The mirrors of the sea are strewn
Between their silver bars!

An isle beside an isle she lay,
The pale ship anchored in the bay,
While in the young moon's port of gold
A star-ship—as the mirrors told—
Put forth its great and lonely light

To the unreflecting Ocean, Night.
And still, a ship upon her seas,
The isle and the island cypresses
Went sailing on without the gale:
And still there moved the moon so pale,
A crescent ship without a sail!

JAMES ELROY FLECKER

The Old Ships

I have seen old ships sail like swans asleep
Beyond the village which men still call Tyre,
With leaden age o'ercargoed, dipping deep
For Famagusta and the hidden sun
That rings black Cyprus with a lake of fire;
And all those ships were certainly so old
Who knows how oft with squat and noisy gun,
Questing brown slaves or Syrian oranges,
The pirate Genoese
Hell-raked them till they rolled
Blood, water, fruit and corpses up the hold.
But now through friendly seas they softly run,
Painted the mid-sea blue or shore-sea green,
Still patterned with the vine and grapes in gold.

But I have seen,
Pointing her shapely shadows from the dawn
And image tumbled on a rose-swept bay,
A drowsy ship of some yet older day;
And, wonder's breath indrawn,
Thought I—who knows—who knows—but in that
(Fished up beyond Ææa, patched up new
—Stern painted brighter blue—)
That talkative, bald-headed seaman came
(Twelve patient comrades sweating at the oar)
From Troy's doom-crimson shore,
And with great lies about his wooden horse
Set the crew laughing, and forgot his course.

It was so old a ship—who knows, who knows?
—And yet so beautiful, I watched in vain
To see the mast burst open with a rose,
And the whole deck put on its leaves again.

JAMES ELROY FLECKER

I Thought of Thee, My Partner and My Guide

I thought of Thee, my partner and my guide
As being past away.—Vain sympathies!
For, backward, Duddon, as I cast my eyes,
I see what was, and is, and will abide;
Still glides the Stream, and shall for ever glide;
The Form remains, the Function never dies;
While we, the brave, the mighty, and the wise,
We Men, who in our morn of youth defied
The elements, must vanish;—be it so!
Enough, if something from our hands have power
To live, and act, and serve the future hour;
And if, as toward the silent tomb we go,
Through love, through hope, and faith's transcendent dower,
We feel that we are greater than we know.

WILLIAM WORDSWORTH

The Ship of Death

I

Now it is autumn and the falling fruit
and the long journey towards oblivion.

The apples falling like great drops of dew
to bruise themselves an exit from themselves.

And it is time to go, to bid farewell
to one's own self, and find an exit
from the fallen self.

[171]

II

Have you built your ship of death, O have you?
O build your ship of death, for you will need it.

The grim frost is at hand, when the apples will fall
thick, almost thundrous, on the hardened earth.

And death is on the air like a smell of ashes!
Ah! can't you smell it?

And in the bruised body, the frightened soul
finds itself shrinking, wincing from the cold
that blows upon it through the orifices.

III

And can a man his own quietus make
with a bare bodkin?

With daggers, bodkins, bullets, man can make
a bruise or break of exit for his life;
but is that a quietus, O tell me, is it quietus?

Surely not so! for how could murder, even self-murder
ever a quietus make?

IV

O let us talk of quiet that we know,
that we can know, the deep and lovely quiet
of a strong heart at peace!

How can we this, our own quietus, make?

V

Build then the ship of death, for you must take
the longest journey, to oblivion.

And die the death, the long and painful death
that lies between the old self and the new.

Already our bodies are fallen, bruised, badly bruised,
already our souls are oozing through the exit
of the cruel bruise.

Already the dark and endless ocean of the end
is washing in through the breaches of our wounds,
already the flood is upon us.

Oh build your ship of death, your little ark
and furnish it with food, with little cakes, and wine
for the dark flight down oblivion.

VI

Piecemeal the body dies, and the timid soul
has her footing washed away, as the dark flood rises.

We are dying, we are dying, we are all of us dying
and nothing will stay the death-flood rising within us
and soon it will rise on the world, on the outside world.

We are dying, we are dying, piecemeal our bodies are dying
and our strength leaves us,
and our soul cowers naked in the dark rain over the flood,
cowering in the last branches of the tree of our life.

VII

We are dying, we are dying, so all we can do
is now to be willing to die, and to build the ship
of death to carry the soul on the longest journey.

A little ship, with oars and food
and little dishes, and all accoutrements
fitting and ready for the departing soul.

Now launch the small ship, now as the body dies
and life departs, launch out, the fragile soul
in the fragile ship of courage, the ark of faith
with its store of food and little cooking pans
and change of clothes,
upon the flood's black waste
upon the waters of the end
upon the sea of death, where still we sail
darkly, for we cannot steer, and have no port.

There is no port, there is nowhere to go
only the deepening blackness darkening still
blacker upon the soundless, ungurgling flood
darkness at one with darkness, up and down
and sideways utterly dark, so there is no direction any more.
and the little ship is there; yet she is gone.
She is not seen, for there is nothing to see her by.
She is gone! gone! and yet
somewhere she is there.
Nowhere!

VIII

And everything is gone, the body is gone
completely under, gone, entirely gone.
The upper darkness is heavy as the lower,
between them the little ship
is gone
she is gone.

It is the end, it is oblivion.

IX

And yet out of eternity, a thread
separates itself on the blackness,
a horizontal thread
that fumes a little with pallor upon the dark.

Is it illusion? or does the pallor fume
A little higher?
Ah wait, wait, for there's the dawn,
the cruel dawn of coming back to life
out of oblivion.

Wait, wait, the little ship
drifting, beneath the deathly ashy grey
of a flood-dawn.

Wait, wait! even so, a flush of yellow
and strangely, O chilled wan soul, a flush of rose.

A flush of rose, and the whole thing starts again.

                            X
The flood subsides, and the body, like a worn sea-shell
emerges strange and lovely.
And the little ship wings home, faltering and lapsing
on the pink flood,
and the frail soul steps out, into her house again
filling the heart with peace.

Swings the heart renewed with peace
even of oblivion.

Oh build your ship of death, oh build it!
for you will need it.
For the voyage of oblivion awaits you.

                                        D. H. LAWRENCE

The Answer

My comforts drop and melt away like snow:
I shake my head, and all the thoughts and ends,
Which my fierce youth did bandie, fall and flow
Like leaves about me: or like summer friends,
Flyes of estates and sunne-shine. But to all,
Who think me eager, hot, and undertaking,
But in my prosecutions slack and small;
As a young exhalation, newly waking,
Scorns his first bed of dirt, and means the sky;
But cooling by the way, grows pursie and slow,
And setling to a cloud, doth live and die
In that dark state of tears: to all, that so
    Show me, and set me, I have one reply,
    Which they that know the rest, know more then I.

GEORGE HERBERT

A Nut, a World, a Squirrel, and a King

Perplex'd with trifles thro' the vale of life,
Man strives 'gainst man, without a cause for strife;
Armies embattled meet, and thousands bleed,
For some vile spot, which cannot fifty feed.
Squirrels for nuts contend, and, wrong or right,
For the world's empire, kings ambitious fight,
What odds?—to us 'tis all the self-same thing,
A Nut, a World, a Squirrel, and a King. . . .

CHARLES CHURCHILL

Wherefore, Unlaurelled Boy

Wherefore, unlaurelled Boy,
    Whom the contemptuous Muse will not inspire,
With a sad kind of joy,
    Still sing'st thou to thy solitary lyre?

[176]

The melancholy winds
    Pour through unnumber'd reeds their idle woes,
And every Naiad finds
    A stream to weep her sorrow as it flows.

Her sighs unto the air
    The wood-maid's native oak doth broadly tell,
And Echo's fond despair
    Intelligible rocks re-syllable.

Wherefore then should not I,
    Albeit no haughty Muse my breast inspire,
Fated of grief to die,
    Impart it to a solitary lyre?

GEORGE DARLEY

Farewell, Sweet Boy

Farewell sweet boy, complain not of my truth;
Thy mother lov'd thee not with more devotion;
For to thy boy's play I gave all my youth,
Young master, I did hope for your promotion.

While some sought honours, princes' thoughts observing,
Many woo'd Fame, the child of pain and anguish,
Others judg'd inward good a chief deserving,
I in thy wanton visions joy'd to languish.

I bow'd not to thy image for succession,
Nor bound thy bow to shoot reformed kindness,
Thy plays of hope and fear were my confession,
The spectacles to my life was thy blindness;
    But Cupid now farewell, I will go play me,
    With thoughts that please me less and less betray me.

FULKE GREVILLE, LORD BROOKE

Timor Mortis Conturbat Me

I that in heill wes and gladnes
Am trublit now with gret seiknes
And feblit with infermite:
Timor mortis conturbat me.

Our plesance heir is all vane glory,
This fals warld is bot transitory,
The flesch is brukle, the Fend is sle:
Timor mortis conturbat me.

The stait of man dois change and vary,
Now sound, now seik, now blith, now sary,
Now dansand mery, now like to dee:
Timor mortis conturbat me.

No stait in erd heir standis sickir;
As with the wynd wavis the wickir
Wavis this warldis vanite:
Timor mortis conturbat me.

One to the ded gois all estatis,
Princis, prelotis and potestatis,
Baith riche and pur of all degre:
Timor mortis conturbat me.

He takis the knychtis in to feild
Anarmyt undir helme and scheild,
Victour he is at all melle:
Timor mortis conturbat me.

That strang unmercifull tyrand
Takis one the moderis breist sowkand
The bab full of benignite:
Timor mortis conturbat me.

He takis the campion in the stour,
The capitane closit in the tour,
The lady in bour full of bewte:
Timor mortis conturbat me.

He sparis no lord for his piscence,
Na clerk for his intelligence;
His awfull strak may no man fle:
Timor mortis conturbat me.

Art magicianis and astrologgis,
Rethoris, logicianis and theologgis—
Thame helpis no conclusionis sle:
Timor mortis conturbat me.

In medicyne the most practicianis,
Lechis, surrigianis and phisicianis,
Thame self fra ded may not supple:
Timor mortis conturbat me.

I se that makaris amang the laif
Playis heir ther pageant, syne gois to graif;
Sparit is nought ther faculte:
Timor mortis conturbat me.

He has done petuously devour
The noble Chaucer of makaris flour,
The monk of Bery, and Gower, all thre:
Timor mortis conturbat me.

The gud Syr Hew of Eglintoun
And eik Heryot and Wyntoun
He has tane out of this cuntre:
Timor mortis conturbat me.

That scorpion fell has done infek
Maister Johne Clerk and James Afflek
Fra balat making the trigide:
Timor mortis conturbat me.

Holland and Barbour he has berevit;
Allace that he nought with us levit
Schir Mungo Lokert of the Le:
Timor mortis conturbat me.

Clerk of Tranent eik he has tane
That maid the anteris of Gawane;
Schir Gilbert Hay endit has he:
Timor mortis conturbat me.

He has Blind Hary and Sandy Traill
Slane with his schour of mortall haill
Quhilk Patrik Johnestoun myght nought fle:
Timor mortis conturbat me.

He has reft Merseir his endite
That did in luf so lifly write,
So schort, so quyk, of sentence hie:
Timor mortis conturbat me.

He has tane Roull of Aberdene
And gentill Roull of Corstorphin—
Two bettir fallowis did no man se:
Timor mortis conturbat me.

In Dunfermelyne he has done roune
With Maister Robert Henrisoun;
Schir Johne the Ros enbrast has he:
Timor mortis conturbat me.

And he has now tane last of aw
Gud gentill Stobo and Quintyne Schaw
Of quham all wichtis has pete:
Timor mortis conturbat me.

Gud Maister Walter Kennedy
In poynt of dede lyis veraly—
Gret reuth it wer that so suld be:
Timor mortis conturbat me.

[180]

Sen he has all my brether tane
He will naught lat me lif alane;
On forse I man his nyxt pray be:
Timor mortis conturbat me.

Sen for the ded remeid is none
Best is that we for dede dispone
Eftir our deid that lif may we:
Timor mortis conturbat me.

WILLIAM DUNBAR

Timor mortis conturbat me:
  The fear of death troubles me
brukle: feeble
sle: cunning
sickir: sure
wickir: willow
potestatis: powers
campion: champion
stour: fight
piscence: puissance
supple: help
makaris: poets
the laif: the rest
infek: rendered incapable
anteris: adventures
endite: writing
dispone: lay out

The Day of Judgement

With a Whirl of Thought oppress'd,
I sink from Reverie to Rest.
An horrid Vision seiz'd my Head,
I saw the Graves give up their Dead.
Jove, arm'd with Terrors, burst the Skies,
And Thunder roars, and Light'ning flies!
Amaz'd, confus'd, its Fate unknown,
The World stands trembling at his Throne.
While each pale Sinner hangs his Head,
Jove nodding, shook the Heav'ns, and said,
"Offending Race of Human Kind,
By Nature, Reason, Learning, blind;
You who thro' Frailty step'd aside,
And you who never fell—*thro' Pride*;
You who in different Sects have shamm'd,
And come to see each other damn'd;
(So some Folks told you, but they knew

[181]

No more of Jove's Designs than you)
The World's mad Business now is o'er,
And I resent these Pranks no more.
I to such Blockheads set my Wit!
I damn such Fools!—Go, go, you're bit.''

JONATHAN SWIFT

Hatred and Vengeance, My Eternal Portion

Hatred and vengeance, my eternal portion,
Scarce can endure delay of execution:—
Wait, with impatient readiness, to seize my
    Soul in a moment.
Damn'd below Judas; more abhorr'd than he was,
Who, for a few pence, sold his holy master.
Twice betray'd, Jesus me, the last delinquent,
    Deems the profanest.
Man disavows, the Deity disowns me.
Hell might afford my miseries a shelter;
Therefore hell keeps her everhungry mouths all
    Bolted against me.
Hard lot! Encompass'd with a thousand dangers,
Weary, faint, trembling with a thousand terrors,
Fall'n, and if vanquish'd, to receive a sentence
    Worse than Abiram's:
Him, the vindictive rod of angry justice
Sent, quick and howling, to the centre headlong;
I, fed with judgements, in a fleshy tomb, am
    Buried above ground.

WILLIAM COWPER

I Am Dead, Horatio

HAMLET:
> I am dead, Horatio. Wretched queen, adieu!
> You that look pale and tremble at this chance,
> That are but mutes or audience to this act,
> Had I but time—as this fell sergeant, Death,
> Is strict in his arrest—O, I could tell you—
> But let it be. Horatio, I am dead;
> Thou livest; report me and my cause aright
> To the unsatisfied.

HORATIO: Never believe it.
> I am more an antique Roman than a Dane.
> Here's yet some liquor left.

HAMLET: As th' art a man,
> Give me the cup. Let go. By heaven, I'll ha't!
> O God, Horatio, what a wounded name,
> Things standing thus unknown, shall live behind me!
> If thou didst ever hold me in thy heart,
> Absent thee from felicity awhile,
> And in this harsh world draw thy breath in pain,
> To tell my story.
> (*A march afar off.*)

                        What warlike noise is this?

OSRIC:
> Young Fortinbras, with conquest come from Poland,
> To the ambassadors of England gives
> This warlike volley.

HAMLET: O, I die, Horatio!
> The potent poison quite o'ercrows my spirit.
> I cannot live to hear the news from England,
> But I do prophesy th'election lights
> On Fortinbras. He has my dying voice.
> So tell him, with th' occurrents, more and less,
> Which have solicited—the rest is silence.
> (*Dies.*)

HORATIO:
> Now cracks a noble heart. Good night, sweet prince,
> And flights of angels sing thee to thy rest!

WILLIAM SHAKESPEARE

Tears, Idle Tears

Tears, idle tears, I know not what they mean,
Tears from the depth of some divine despair
Rise in the heart, and gather to the eyes,
In looking on the happy Autumn-fields,
And thinking of the days that are no more.

Fresh as the first beam glittering on a sail,
That brings our friends up from the underworld,
Sad as the last which reddens over one
That sinks with all we love below the verge;
So sad, so fresh, the days that are no more.

Ah, sad and strange as in dark summer dawns
The earliest pipe of half-awaken'd birds
To dying ears, when unto dying eyes
The casement slowly grows a glimmering square;
So sad, so strange, the days that are no more.

Dear as remember'd kisses after death,
And sweet as those by hopeless fancy feign'd
On lips that are for others; deep as love,
Deep as first love, and wild with all regret;
O Death in Life, the days that are no more.

ALFRED TENNYSON

Come Not when I Am Dead

Come not, when I am dead,
  To drop thy foolish tears upon my grave,
To trample round my fallen head,
  And vex the unhappy dust thou wouldst not save.
There let the wind sweep and the plover cry;
        But thou, go by.

Child, if it were thine error or thy crime
    I care no longer, being all unblest:
Wed whom thou wilt, but I am sick of Time,
    And I desire to rest.
Pass on, weak heart, and leave me where I lie:
        Go by, go by.

ALFRED TENNYSON

When, in Disgrace with Fortune
and Men's Eyes

When, in disgrace with Fortune and men's eyes,
I all alone beweep my outcast state,
And trouble deaf heaven with my bootless cries,
And look upon myself and curse my fate,
Wishing me like to one more rich in hope,
Featured like him, like him with friends possessed,
Desiring this man's art, and that man's scope,
With what I most enjoy contented least;
Yet in these thoughts myself almost despising,
Haply I think on thee, and then my state,
Like to the lark at break of day arising
From sullen earth, sings hymns at heaven's gate;
    For thy sweet love rememb'red such wealth brings
    That then I scorn to change my state with kings.

WILLIAM SHAKESPEARE

Avarice

Money, thou bane of blisse, and sourse of wo,
    Whence com'st thou, that thou art so fresh and fine?
    I know thy parentage is base and low:
Man found thee poore and dirtie in a mine.
Surely thou didst so little contribute
    To this great kingdome, which thou now hast got,
    That he was fain, when thou wert destitute,

To digge thee out of thy dark cave and grot:
Then forcing thee by fire he made thee bright:
   Nay, thou hast got the face of man; for we
   Have with our stamp and seal transferr'd our right:
Thou art the man, and man but drosse to thee.
   Man calleth thee his wealth, who made thee rich;
   And while he digs out thee, falls in the ditch.

GEORGE HERBERT

Barmenissa's Song

The stately state that wise men count their good:
The chiefest bliss that lulls asleep desire
Is not descent from kings and princely blood,
Ne stately Crown ambition doth require,
   For birth by fortune is abased down,
   And perils are comprised within a Crown.

The Sceptre and the glittering pomp of mace,
The head impaled with honour and renown,
The Kingly throne, the seat and regal place,
Are toys that fade when angry fortune frown.
   Content is far from such delights as those,
   Whom woe and danger do envy as foes.

The Cottage seated in the hollow dale,
That fortune never fears, because so low,
The quiet mind that want doth set to sale
Sleeps safe when Princes seats do overthrow.
   Want smiles secure, when princely thoughts do feel
   That fear and danger treads upon their heel.

Bless fortune thou whose frown hath wrought thy good:
Bid farewell to the Crown that ends thy care,
The happy fates thy sorrows have withstood,
By signing want and poverty thy share.
   For now content (fond fortune to despite)
   With patience lows thee quiet and delight.

ROBERT GREENE

The Magi

Now as at all times I can see in the mind's eye,
In their stiff, painted clothes, the pale unsatisfied ones
Appear and disappear in the blue depth of the sky
With all their ancient faces like rain-beaten stones,
And all their helms of silver hovering side by side,
And all their eyes still fixed, hoping to find once more,
Being by Calvary's turbulence unsatisfied,
The uncontrollable mystery on the bestial floor.

W. B. YEATS

Under Bare Ben Bulben's Head

Under bare Ben Bulben's head
In Drumcliff churchyard Yeats is laid.
An ancestor was rector there
Long years ago, a church stands near,
By the road an ancient cross.
No marble, no conventional phrase;
On limestone quarried near the spot
By his command these words are cut:

> *Cast a cold eye*
> *On life, on death.*
> *Horseman, pass by!*

W. B. YEATS

Be Absolute for Death

Be absolute for death: either death or life
Shall thereby be the sweeter. Reason thus with life:
If I do lose thee, I do lose a thing
That none but fools would keep; a breath thou art,
Servile to all the skyey influences
That dost this habitation where thou keep'st
Hourly afflict; merely, thou art death's fool,

[187]

For him thou labor'st by thy flight to shun,
And yet run'st toward him still. Thou art not noble,
For all th'accommodations that thou bear'st
Are nursed by baseness. Thou'rt by no means valiant,
For thou dost fear the soft and tender fork
Of a poor worm; thy best of rest is sleep,
And that thou oft provok'st, yet grossly fear'st
Thy death, which is no more. Thou art not thyself,
For thou exists on many a thousand grains
That issue out of dust. Happy thou art not,
For what thou hast not, still thou striv'st to get,
And what thou hast, forget'st. Thou art not certain,
For thy complexion shifts to strange effects,
After the moon. If thou art rich, thou'rt poor,
For, like an ass whose back with ingots bows,
Thou bear'st thy heavy riches but a journey,
And death unloads thee. Friend hast thou none,
For thine own bowels, which do call thee sire,
The mere effusion of thy proper loins,
Do curse the gout, serpigo, and the rheum
For ending thee no sooner. Thou hast nor youth nor age,
But as it were an after-dinner's sleep,
Dreaming on both, for all thy blessèd youth
Becomes as agèd, and doth beg the alms
Of palsied eld: and when thou art old and rich,
Thou hast neither heat, affection, limb, nor beauty,
To make thy riches pleasant. What's yet in this
That bears the name of life? Yet in this life
Lie hid moe thousand deaths; yet death we fear,
That makes these odds all even.

WILLIAM SHAKESPEARE

There Rolls the Deep

There rolls the deep where grew the tree.
    O earth, what changes hast thou seen!
    There where the long street roars, hath been
The stillness of the central sea.

The hills are shadows, and they flow
  From form to form, and nothing stands;
  They melt like mist, the solid lands,
Like clouds they shape themselves and go.

But in my spirit will I dwell,
  And dream my dream, and hold it true;
  For though my lips may breathe adieu,
I cannot think the thing farewell.

ALFRED TENNYSON

When to the Sessions of Sweet Silent Thought

When to the sessions of sweet silent thought
I summon up remembrance of things past,
I sigh the lack of many a thing I sought,
And with old woes new wail my dear time's waste:
Then can I drown an eye, unused to flow,
For precious friends hid in death's dateless night,
And weep afresh love's long since cancelled woe,
And moan th'expense of many a vanished sight.
Then can I grieve at grievances foregone,
And heavily from woe to woe tell o'er
The sad account of fore-bemoanèd moan,
Which I new pay as if not paid before.
  But if the while I think on thee, dear friend,
  All losses are restored and sorrows end.

WILLIAM SHAKESPEARE

The Glories of Our Blood
and State

The glories of our blood and state,
   Are shadows, not substantial things,
There is no armour against fate,
   Death lays his icy hand on Kings,
       Scepter and Crown,
       Must tumble down,
And in the dust be equal made,
With the poor crooked sithe and spade.

Some men with swords may reap the field,
   And plant fresh laurels where they kill,
But their strong nerves at last must yield,
   They tame but one another still;
       Early or late,
       They stoop to fate,
And must give up the murmuring breath,
When they pale Captives creep to death.

The Garlands wither on your brow,
   Then boast no more your mighty deeds,
Upon Deaths purple Altar now,
   See where the Victor-victim bleeds,
       Your heads must come,
       To the cold Tomb;
Onely the actions of the just
Smell sweet, and blossom in their dust.

JAMES SHIRLEY

Wolsey

Cromwell, I did not think to shed a tear
In all my miseries; but thou hast forced me
(Out of thy honest truth) to play the woman.
Let's dry our eyes: and thus far hear me, Cromwell,
And when I am forgotten, as I shall be,

And sleep in dull cold marble, where no mention
Of me more must be heard of, say I taught thee;
Say, Wolsey, that once trod the ways of glory
And sounded all the depths and shoals of honor,
Found thee a way (out of his wrack) to rise in,
A sure and safe one, though thy master missed it.
Mark but my fall and that that ruined me.
Cromwell, I charge thee, fling away ambition!
By that sin fell the angels; how can man then
(The image of his Maker) hope to win by it?
Love thyself last, cherish those hearts that hate thee;
Corruption wins not more than honesty.
Still in thy right hand carry gentle peace
To silence envious tongues. Be just, and fear not.
Let all the ends thou aim'st at be thy country's,
Thy God's and truth's: then if thou fall'st, O Cromwell,
Thou fall'st a blessed martyr.
Serve the king. And prithee lead me in:
There take an inventory of all I have
To the last penny: 'tis the king's. My robe,
And my integrity to heaven, is all
I dare now call mine own. O Cromwell, Cromwell,
Had I but served my God with half the zeal
I served my king, he would not in mine age
Have left me naked to mine enemies.

WILLIAM SHAKESPEARE

Ozymandias

I met a traveller from an antique land
Who said: Two vast and trunkless legs of stone
Stand in the desert. Near them, on the sand,
Half sunk, a shattered visage lies, whose frown,
And wrinkled lip, and sneer of cold command,
Tell that its sculptor well those passions read
Which yet survive, stamped on these lifeless things,
The hand that mocked them, and the heart that fed:
And on the pedestal these words appear:

[191]

"My name is Ozymandias, king of kings:
Look on my works, ye Mighty, and despair!"
Nothing beside remains. Round the decay
Of that colossal wreck, boundless and bare
The lone and level sands stretch far away.

PERCY BYSSHE SHELLEY

To the Driving Cloud

Gloomy and dark art thou, O chief of the mighty Omahas;
Gloomy and dark, as the driving cloud, whose name thou hast taken!
Wrapt in thy scarlet blanket, I see thee stalk through the city's
Narrow and populous streets, as once by the margin of rivers
Stalked those birds unknown, that have left us only their footprints.
What, in a few short years, will remain of thy race but the footprints?

How canst thou walk these streets, who hast trod the green turf of the
    prairies?
How canst thou breathe this air, who hast breathed the sweet air of
    the mountains?
Ah! 'tis in vain that with lordly looks of disdain thou dost challenge
Looks of disdain in return, and question these walls and these
    pavements,
Claiming the soil for thy hunting-grounds, while down-trodden
    millions
Starve in the garrets of Europe, and cry from its caverns that they, too,
Have been created heirs of the earth, and claim its division!

Back, then, back to thy woods in the regions west of the Wabash!
There as a monarch thou reignest. In autumn the leaves of the maple
Pave the floors of thy palace-halls with gold, and in summer
Pine-trees waft through its chambers the odorous breath of their
    branches.
There thou art strong and great, a hero, a tamer of horses!
There thou chasest the stately stag on the banks of the Elk-horn,
Or by the roar of the Running-Water, or where the Omawhaw
Calls thee, and leaps through the wild ravine like a brave of the
    Blackfeet!

[192]

Hark! what murmurs arise from the heart of those mountainous
    deserts?
Is it the cry of the Foxes and Crows, or the mighty Behemoth,
Who, unharmed, on his tusks once caught the bolts of the thunder,
And now lurks in his lair to destroy the race of the red man?
Far more fatal to thee and thy race than the Crows and the Foxes,
Far more fatal to thee and thy race than the tread of Behemoth,
Lo! the big thunder-canoe, that steadily breasts the Missouri's
Merciless current! and yonder, afar on the prairies, the camp-fires
Gleam through the night; and the cloud of dust in the grey of the
    daybreak
Marks not the buffalo's track, nor the Mandan's dexterous horse-race;
It is a caravan, whitening the desert where dwell the Camanches!
Ha! how the breath of these Saxons and Celts, like the blast of the
    east-wind,
Drifts evermore to the west the scanty smokes of thy wigwams!

H. W. LONGFELLOW

By the Statue of King Charles
at Charing Cross

Sombre and rich, the skies;
Great glooms, and starry plains.
Gently the night wind sighs;
Else a vast silence reigns.

The splendid silence clings
Around me: and around
The saddest of all kings
Crowned, and again discrowned.

Comely and calm, he rides
Hard by his own Whitehall:
Only the night wind glides:
No crowds, nor rebels, brawl.

Gone, too, his Court: and yet,
The stars his courtiers are:
Stars in their stations set;
And every wandering star.

Alone he rides, alone,
The fair and fatal king:
Dark night is all his own,
That strange and solemn thing.

Which are more full of fate:
The stars; or those sad eyes?
Which are more still and great:
Those brows; or the dark skies?

Although his whole heart yearn
In passionate tragedy:
Never was face so stern
With sweet austerity.

Vanquished in life, his death
By beauty made amends:
The passing of his breath
Won his defeated ends.

LIONEL JOHNSON

King Charles
on the Scaffold

He nothing common did or mean
Upon that memorable scene:
  But with his keener eye
  The axe's edge did try:
Nor called the gods with vulgar spite
To vindicate his helpless right,
  But bowed his comely head,
  Down, as upon a bed.

ANDREW MARVELL

Life

I made a posie, while the day ran by:
Here will I smell my remnant out, and tie
              My life within this band.
But Time did beckon to the flowers, and they
By noon most cunningly did steal away,
              And wither'd in my hand.

My hand was next to them, and then my heart:
I took, without more thinking, in good part
              Times gentle admonition:
Who did so sweetly deaths sad taste convey,
Making my minde to smell my fatall day;
              Yet sugring the suspicion.

Farewell deare flowers, sweetly your time ye spent,
Fit, while ye liv'd, for smell or ornament,
              And after death for cures.
I follow straight without complaints or grief,
Since if my sent be good, I care not if
              It be as short as yours.

GEORGE HERBERT

The Tuft of Kelp

    All dripping in tangles green,
      Cast up by a lonely sea,
   If purer for that, O Weed,
      Bitterer, too, are ye?

HERMAN MELVILLE

Against the Fear of Death

I

Ah Wretch! thou cry'st, ah! miserable me;
One woful day sweeps children, friends, and wife,
And all the brittle blessings of my life!
Add one thing more, and all thou say'st is true:
Thy want and wish of them is vanish'd too:
Which, well consider'd, were a quick relief,
To all thy vain imaginary grief.
For thou shalt sleep, and never wake again,
And, quitting life, shalt quit thy living pain.
But we, thy friends, shall all those sorrows find,
Which in forgetful death thou leav'st behind;
No time shall dry our tears, nor drive thee from our mind.
The worst that can befall thee, measur'd right,
Is a sound slumber, and a long good night.

II

So many Monarchs with their mighty State,
Who rul'd the World, were over-rul'd by fate.
That haughty King, who lorded o'er the Main,
And whose stupendous Bridge did the wild Waves restrain,
(In vain they foam'd, in vain they threatned wreck,
While his proud Legions march'd upon their back:)
Him death, a greater Monarch, overcame;
Not spar'd his guards the more, for their immortal name.
The *Roman* chief, the *Carthaginian* dread,
Scipio, the Thunder Bolt of War, is dead,
And like a common Slave, by fate in triumph led.
The Founders of invented Arts are lost;
And Wits who made Eternity their boast.
Where now is *Homer*, who possest the Throne?
Th'immortal Work remains, the mortal Author's gone.
Democritus, perceiving age invade,
His Body weakn'd, and his mind decay'd,
Obey'd the summons with a cheerful face;
Made hast to welcom death, and met him half the race.
That stroke ev'n *Epicurus* cou'd not bar,
Though he in Wit surpass'd Mankind as far

As does the midday Sun the midnight Star.
And thou, dost thou disdain to yield thy breath,
Whose very Life is little more than Death?
More than one half by Lazy sleep possest;
And when awake, thy Soul but nods at best,
Day-Dreams and sickly thoughts revolving in thy breast.
Eternal troubles haunt thy anxious mind,
Whose cause and cure thou never hopst to find;
But still uncertain, with thyself at strife,
Thou wander'st in the *Labyrinth* of Life.
O! if the foolish race of man, who find
A weight of cares still pressing on their mind,
Cou'd find as well the cause of this unrest,
And all this burden lodg'd within the breast;
Sure they wou'd change their course, nor live as now,
Uncertain what to wish or what to vow.
Uneasie both in Countrey and in Town,
They search a place to lay their burden down.
One, restless in his Palace, walks abroad,
And vainly thinks to leave behind the load:
But straight returns; for he's as restless there:
And finds there's no relief in open Air.
Another to his *Villa* wou'd retire,
And spurs as hard as if it were on fire;
No sooner enter'd at his Country door,
But he begins to stretch, and yawn, and snore;
Or seeks the City which he left before.
Thus every man o're works his weary Will,
To shun himself, and to shake off his ill:
The shaking Fit returns, and hangs upon him still.
No prospect of repose, nor hope of ease;
The Wretch is ignorant of his disease;
Which known wou'd all his fruitless trouble spare;
For he wou'd know the World not worth his care;
Then wou'd he search more deeply for the cause;
And study Nature well, and Natures Laws:
For in this moment lies not the debate,
But on our future, fix'd, Eternal State;
That never changing state, which all must keep,
Whom Death has doom'd to everlasting sleep.

Why are we then so fond of mortal Life,
Beset with dangers, and maintain'd with strife?
A Life, which all our care can never save;
One Fate attends us; and one common Grave.
Besides, we tread but a perpetual round;
We ne're strike out, but beat the former ground,
And the same Maukish joyes in the same track are found.
For still we think an absent blessing best,
Which cloys, and is no blessing when possest;
A new arising wish expells it from the Breast.
The Feav'rish thirst of Life increases still;
We call for more and more, and never have our fill;
Yet know not what to-morrow we shall try,
What dregs of life in the last draught may lie:
Nor, by the longest life we can attain,
One moment from the length of death we gain;
For all behind belongs to his Eternal reign.
When once the Fates have cut the mortal Thred,
The Man as much to all intents is dead,
Who dyes to-day, and will as long be so,
As he who dy'd a thousand years ago.

JOHN DRYDEN
(*after* Lucretius)

Paroles sur la Dune

Maintenant que mon temps décroît comme un flambeau,
    Que mes tâches sont terminées;
Maintenant que voici que je touche au tombeau
    Par les deuils et par les années,

Et qu'au fond de ce ciel que mon essor rêva,
    Je vois fuir, vers l'ombre entraînées,
Comme le tourbillon du passé qui s'en va,
    Tant de belles heures sonnées;

Maintenant que je dis:—Un jour, nous triomphons;
    Le lendemain, tout est mensonge!—
Je suis triste, et je marche au bord des flots profonds,
    Courbé comme celui qui songe.

Je regarde, au-dessus du mont et du vallon,
    Et des mers sans fin remuées,
S'envoler sous le bec du vautour aquilon,
    Toute la toison des nuées;

J'entends le vent dans l'air, la mer sur le récif,
    L'homme liant la gerbe mûre;
J'écoute, et je confronte en mon esprit pensif
    Ce qui parle à ce qui murmure;

Et je reste parfois couché sans me lever
    Sur l'herbe rare de la dune,
Jusqu'à l'heure où l'on voit apparaître et rêver
    Les yeux sinistres de la lune.

Elle monte, elle jette un long rayon dormant
    A l'espace, au mystère, au gouffre;
Et nous nous regardons tous les deux fixement,
    Elle qui brille et moi qui souffre.

Où donc s'en sont allés mes jours évanouis?
    Est-il quelqu'un qui me connaisse?
Ai-je encor quelque chose en mes yeux éblouis,
    De la clarté de ma jeunesse?

Tout s'est-il envolé? Je suis seul, je suis las;
    J'appelle sans qu'on me réponde;
O vents! ô flots! ne suis-je aussi qu'un souffle, hélas!
    Hélas! ne suis-je aussi qu'une onde?

Ne verrai-je plus rien de tout ce que j'aimais?
    Au dedans de moi le soir tombe.
O terre, dont la brume efface les sommets,
    Suis-je le spectre, et toi la tombe?

Ai-je donc vidé tout, vie, amour, joie, espoir?
   J'attends, je demande, j'implore;
Je penche tour à tour mes urnes pour avoir
   De chacune une goutte encore!

Comme le souvenir est voisin du remord!
   Comme à pleurer tout nous ramène!
Et que je te sens froide en te touchant, ô mort,
   Noir verrou de la porte humaine!

Et je pense, écoutant gémir le vent amer,
   Et l'onde aux plis infranchissables;
L'été rit, et l'on voit sur le bord de la mer
   Fleurir le chardon bleu des sables.

VICTOR HUGO

Demain dès l'Aube

Demain, dès l'aube, à l'heure où blanchit la campagne,
Je partirai. Vois-tu, je sais que tu m'attends.
J'irai par la forêt, j'irai par la montagne.
Je ne puis demeurer loin de toi plus longtemps.

Je marcherai les yeux fixés sur mes pensées,
Sans rien voir au dehors, sans entendre aucun bruit,
Seul, inconnu, le dos courbé, les mains croisées,
Triste, et le jour pour moi sera comme la nuit.

Je ne regarderai ni l'or du soir qui tombe,
Ni les voiles au loin descendant vers Harfleur,
Et quand j'arriverai, je mettrai sur ta tombe
Un bouquet de houx vert et de bruyère en fleur.

VICTOR HUGO

Leave Me, O Love

Leave me, O Love, which reachest but to dust,
And thou my mind aspire to higher things:
Grow rich in that which never taketh rust:
What ever fades, but fading pleasure brings.
Draw in thy beames, and humble all thy might,
To that sweet yoke, where lasting freedomes be:
Which breakes the clowdes and opens forth the light,
That doth both shine and give us sight to see.
O take fast hold, let that light be thy guide,
In this small course which birth drawes out to death,
And thinke how evill becommeth him to slide,
Who seeketh heav'n, and comes of heav'nly breath.
  Then farewell world, thy uttermost I see,
  Eternall Love maintaine thy life in me.

Splendidis longum valedico nugis.

SIR PHILIP SIDNEY

Over the Dark World Flies
the Wind

Over the dark world flies the wind
  And clatters in the sapless trees,
From cloud to cloud through darkness blind
  Quick stars scud o'er the sounding seas:
I look: the showery skirts unbind:
  Mars by the lonely Pleiades
Burns overhead: with brows declined
  I muse: I wander from my peace,
And still divide the rapid mind
  This way and that in search of ease.

ALFRED TENNYSON

A Farewell

Flow down, cold rivulet, to the sea,
　　Thy tribute wave deliver:
No more by thee my steps shall be,
　　For ever and for ever.

Flow, softly flow, by lawn and lea,
　　A rivulet then a river:
No where by thee my steps shall be,
　　For ever and for ever.

But here will sigh thine alder tree,
　　And here thine aspen shiver;
And here by thee will hum the bee,
　　For ever and for ever.

A thousand suns will stream on thee,
　　A thousand moons will quiver;
But not by thee my steps shall be,
　　For ever and for ever.

ALFRED TENNYSON

On the Extinction of the Venetian Republic

Once did She hold the gorgeous east in fee;
And was the safeguard of the west: the worth
Of Venice did not fall below her birth,
Venice, the eldest Child of Liberty.
She was a maiden City, bright and free;
No guile seduced, no force could violate;
And, when she took unto herself a Mate,
She must espouse the everlasting Sea.
And what if she had seen those glories fade,
Those titles vanish, and that strength decay;
Yet shall some tribute of regret be paid
When her long life hath reached its final day:
Men are we, and must grieve when even the Shade
Of that which once was great, is passed away.

WILLIAM WORDSWORTH

ODE

Intimations of Immortality from Recollections
of Early Childhood

The Child is father of the Man;
And I could wish my days to be
Bound each to each by natural piety.

I

There was a time when meadow, grove, and stream,
   The earth, and every common sight,
         To me did seem
      Apparelled in celestial light,
The glory and the freshness of a dream.
It is not now as it hath been of yore;—
      Turn wheresoe'er I may,
        By night or day,
The things which I have seen I now can see no more.

II

      The Rainbow comes and goes,
      And lovely is the Rose,
      The Moon doth with delight
   Look round her when the heavens are bare,
      Waters on a starry night
      Are beautiful and fair;
    The sunshine is a glorious birth;
    But yet I know, where'er I go,
That there hath past away a glory from the earth.

III

Now, while the birds thus sing a joyous song,
     And while the young lambs bound
      As to the tabor's sound,
To me alone there came a thought of grief:
A timely utterance gave that thought relief,
     And I again am strong:
The cataracts blow their trumpets from the steep;
No more shall grief of mine the season wrong;
I hear the Echoes through the mountains throng,
The Winds come to me from the fields of sleep,

And all the earth is gay;
        Land and sea
Give themselves up to jollity,
        And with the heart of May
Doth every Beast keep holiday;—
        Thou Child of Joy,
Shout round me, let me hear thy shouts, thou happy Shepherd-boy!

                    IV

Ye blessèd Creatures, I have heard the call
        Ye to each other make; I see
The heavens laugh with you in your jubilee;
        My heart is at your festival,
        My head hath its coronal,
The fulness of your bliss, I feel—I feel it all.
        Oh evil day! if I were sullen
        While Earth herself is adorning,
            This sweet May-morning,
        And the Children are culling
            On every side,
        In a thousand valleys far and wide,
        Fresh flowers; while the sun shines warm,
And the Babe leaps up on his Mother's arm:—
        I hear, I hear, with joy I hear!
        —But there's a Tree of many, one,
A single Field which I have looked upon,
Both of them speak of something that is gone:
        The Pansy at my feet
        Doth the same tale repeat:
Whither is fled the visionary gleam?
Where is it now, the glory and the dream?

                    V

Our birth is but a sleep and a forgetting:
The Soul that rises with us, our life's Star,
        Hath had elsewhere its setting,
            And cometh from afar:
        Not in entire forgetfulness,
        And not in utter nakedness,
But trailing clouds of glory do we come

From God, who is our home:
Heavens lies about us in our infancy!
Shades of the prison-house begin to close
    Upon the growing Boy,
But He beholds the light, and whence it flows,
    He sees it in his joy;
The Youth, who daily farther from the east
    Must travel, still is Nature's Priest,
    And by the vision splendid
    Is on his way attended;
At length the Man perceives it die away,
And fade into the light of common day.

VI

Earth fills her lap with pleasures of her own;
Yearnings she hath in her own natural kind,
And, even with something of a Mother's mind,
    And no unworthy aim
    The homely Nurse doth all she can
To make her Foster-child, her Inmate Man,
    Forget the glories he hath known,
And that imperial palace whence he came.

VII

Behold the Child among his new-born blisses,
A six years' Darling of a pigmy size!
See, where 'mid work of his own hand he lies.
Fretted by sallies of his mother's kisses,
With light upon him from his father's eyes!
See, at his feet, some little plan or chart,
Some fragment from his dream of human life,
Shaped by himself with newly-learned art;
    A wedding or a festival,
    A mourning or a funeral;
      And this hath now his heart,
    And unto this he frames his song:
      Then will he fit his tongue
To dialogues of business, love, or strife;
    But it will not be long
    Ere this be thrown aside,

And with new joy and pride
The little Actor cons another part;
Filling from time to time his "humorous stage"
With all the Persons, down to palsied Age,
That Life brings with her in her equipage;
    As if his whole vocation
    Where endless imitation.

VIII

Thou, whose exterior semblance doth belie
    Thy Soul's immensity;
Thou best Philosopher, who yet dost keep
Thy heritage, thou Eye among the blind,
That, deaf and silent, read'st the eternal deep,
Haunted for ever by the eternal mind,—
    Mighty Prophet! Seer blest!
    On whom those truths do rest,
Which we are toiling all our lives to find,
In darkness lost, the darkness of the grave;
Thou, over whom thy Immortality
Broods like the Day, a Master o'er a Slave,
A Presence which is not to be put by;
Thou little Child, yet glorious in the might
Of heaven-born freedom on thy being's height,
Why with such earnest pains dost thou provoke
The years to bring the inevitable yoke,
Thus blindly with thy blessedness at strife?
Full soon thy Soul shall have her earthly freight,
And custom lie upon thee with a weight,
Heavy as frost, and deep almost as life!

IX

    O joy! that in our embers
    Is something that doth live,
    That nature yet remembers
    What was so fugitive!
The thought of our past years in me doth breed
Perpetual benediction: not indeed
For that which is most worthy to be blest—
Delight and liberty, the simple creed

Of Childhood, whether busy or at rest,
With new-fledged hope still fluttering in his breast:—
     Not for these I raise
       The song of thanks and praise;
   But for those obstinate questionings
   Of sense and outward things,
   Fallings from us, vanishings;
   Blank misgivings of a Creature
Moving about in worlds not realized,
High instincts before which our mortal Nature
Did tremble like a guilty Thing surprised:
     But for those first affections,
       Those shadowy recollections,
   Which, be they what they may,
Are yet the fountain light of all our day,
Are yet a master light of all our seeing;
   Uphold us, cherish, and have power to make
Our noisy years seem moments in the being
Of the eternal Silence: truths that wake,
     To perish never;
Which neither listlessness, nor mad endeavour,
     Nor Man nor Boy,
Nor all that is at enmity with joy,
Can utterly abolish or destroy!
     Hence in a season of calm weather
       Though inland far we be,
Our Souls have sight of that immortal sea
     Which brought us hither,
       Can in a moment travel thither,
And see the Children sport upon the shore,
And hear the mighty waters rolling evermore.

X

Then sing, ye Birds, sing, sing a joyous song!
     And let the young Lambs bound
       As to the tabor's sound!
We in thought will join your throng,
     Ye that pipe and ye that play,
       Ye that through your hearts to-day
       Feel the gladness of the May!

[207]

What though the radiance which was once so bright
Be now for ever taken from my sight,
   Though nothing can bring back the hour
Of splendour in the grass, of glory in the flower;
      We will grieve not, rather find
      Strength in what remains behind;
      In the primal sympathy
      Which having been must ever be;
      In the soothing thoughts that spring
      Out of human suffering;
      In the faith that looks through death,
In years that bring the philosophic mind.

XI

And O, ye Fountains, Meadows, Hills, and Groves,
Forebode not any severing of our loves!
Yet in my heart of hearts I feel your might
I only have relinquished one delight
To live beneath your more habitual sway.
I love the Brooks which down their channels fret,
Even more than when I tripped lightly as they;
The innocent brightness of a new-born Day
            Is lovely yet;
The Clouds that gather round the setting sun
Do take a sober colouring from an eye
That hath kept watch o'er man's mortality;
Another race hath been, and other palms are won.
Thanks to the human heart by which we live,
Thanks to its tenderness, its joys, and fears,
To me the meanest flower that blows can give
Thoughts that do often lie too deep for tears.

WILLIAM WORDSWORTH

From the Welsh of Aneirín

In March birds couple, a new birth
Of herbs and flowers breaks through the earth,
But in the grave none stirs his head;
Long is th' Impris'ment of the dead.

HENRY VAUGHAN

Angels Are Bright

Angels are bright still, though the brightest fell.

WILLIAM SHAKESPEARE

Dull, Sullen Prisoners

Most souls, 'tis true, but peep out once an age,
Dull sullen pris'ners in the body's cage:
Dim lights of life that burn a length of years,
Useless, unseen, as lamps in sepulchres;
Like Eastern Kings a lazy state they keep,
And close confin'd to their own palace sleep.

ALEXANDER POPE

from *Prometheus Unbound*

DEMOGORGON
Thou, Earth, calm empire of a happy soul,
  Sphere of divinest shapes and harmonies,
Beautiful orb! gathering as thou dost roll
  The love which paves thy path along the skies:

THE EARTH
I hear: I am as a drop of dew that dies.

Thou, Moon, which gazest on the nightly Earth
  With wonder, as it gazes upon thee;
Whilst each to men, and beasts, and the swift birth
  Of birds, is beauty, love, calm, harmony:

THE MOON

  I hear: I am a leaf shaken by thee!

DEMOGORGON

Ye kings of suns and stars, Daemons and Gods,
  Aetherial Dominations, who possess
Elysian, windless, fortunate abodes
  Beyond Heaven's constellated wilderness:

A VOICE FROM ABOVE

  Our great Republic hears, we are blest, and bless.

DEMOGORGON

Ye happy dead, whom beams of brightest verse
  Are clouds to hide, not colours to pourtray,
Whether your nature is that universe
  Which once ye saw and suffered—

A VOICE FROM BENEATH

                                                  Or as they
  Whom we have left, we change and pass away.

DEMOGORGON

Ye elemental Genii, who have homes
  From man's high mind even to the central stone
Of sullen lead; from Heaven's star-fretted domes
  To the dull weed some sea-worm battens on:

A CONFUSED VOICE

We hear: thy words waken Oblivion.

DEMOGORGON

Spirits, whose homes are flesh: ye beasts and birds,
  Ye worms, and fish; ye living leaves and buds;
Lightning and wind; and ye untameable herds,
  Meteors and mists, which throng air's solitudes:

A VOICE

  Thy voice to us is wind among still woods.

DEMOGORGON

Man, who wert once a despot and a slave;
  A dupe and a deceiver; a decay;
A traveller from the cradle to the grave
  Through the dim night of this immortal day:

ALL

  Speak: thy strong words may never pass away.

DEMOGORGON

This is the day, which down the void abysm
At the Earth-born's spell yawns for Heaven's despotism,
  And Conquest is dragged captive through the deep:
Love, from its awful throne of patient power
In the wise heart, from the last giddy hour
  Of dread endurance, from the slippery, steep,
And narrow verge of crag-like agony, springs
And folds over the world its healing wings.

Gentleness, Virtue, Wisdom, and Endurance,
These are the seals of that most firm assurance
  Which bars the pit over Destruction's strength;
And if, with infirm hand, Eternity,
Mother of many acts and hours, should free
  The serpent that would clasp her with his length;
These are the spells by which to re-assume
An empire o'er the disentangled doom.

To suffer woes which Hope thinks infinite;
To forgive wrongs darker than death or night;
   To defy Power, which seems omnipotent;
To love, and bear; to hope till Hope creates
From its own wreck the thing it contemplates;
   Neither to change, nor faulter, nor repent;
This, like thy glory, Titan, is to be
Good, great and joyous, beautiful and free;
This is alone Life, Joy, Empire, and Victory.

PERCY BYSSHE SHELLEY

Dark Churches

   Churches are best for prayer, that have least light:
   To see God only, I go out of sight:
     And to 'scape stormy days, I choose
      An everlasting night.

JOHN DONNE

At the Round Earth's Imagin'd Corners

At the round earths imagin'd corners, blow
Your trumpets, Angells, and arise, arise
From death, you numberlesse infinities
Of soules, and to your scattred bodies goe,
All whom the flood did, and fire shall o'erthrow,
All whom warre, dearth, age, agues, tyrannies,
Despaire, law, chance, hath slaine, and you whose eyes,
Shall behold God, and never tast deaths woe.
But let them sleepe, Lord, and mee mourne a space,
For, if above all these, my sinnes abound,
'Tis late to aske abundance of thy grace,
When wee are there; here on this lowly ground,
Teach mee how to repent; for that's as good
As if thou hadst seal'd my pardon, with thy blood.

JOHN DONNE

After Dark Vapours

After dark vapours have oppress'd our plains
   For a long dreary season, comes a day
   Born of the gentle South, and clears away
From the sick heavens all unseemly stains.
The anxious month, relieving from its pains,
   Takes as a long-lost right the feel of May,
   The eyelids with the passing coolness play,
Like rose leaves with the drip of summer rains.
The calmest thoughts come round us—as of leaves
   Budding,—fruit ripening in stillness,—autumn suns
Smiling at eve upon the quiet sheaves,—
Sweet Sappho's cheek,—a sleeping infant's breath,—
   The gradual sand that through an hour-glass runs,—
A woodland rivulet,—a Poet's death.

JOHN KEATS

His Epitaph
Which He Writ the Night Before
His Execution

Even such is time that takes in trust
Our youth, our joys, and all we have,
And pays us but with age and dust:
Who in the dark and silent grave
When we have wandred all our ways
Shuts up the story of our days.
And from which earth and grave and dust
The Lord shall raise me up, I trust.

SIR WALTER RALEGH

The Sun May Set

The sun may set and rise:
But we contrariwise
Sleep after our short light
One everlasting night.

SIR WALTER RALEGH
(*after* Catullus)

What Are Heavy?

What are heavy? sea-sand and sorrow:
What are brief? to-day and to-morrow:
What are frail? Spring blossoms and youth:
What are deep? the ocean and truth.

CHRISTINA ROSSETTI

Lyrick for Legacies

Gold I've none, for use or show,
Neither Silver to bestow
At my death; but thus much know,
That each Lyrick here shall be
Of my love a Legacie,
Left to all posterity.
Gentle friends, then doe but please,
To accept such coynes as these;
As my last Remembrances.

ROBERT HERRICK

The Old Summerhouse

This blue-washed, old, thatched summerhouse—
Paint scaling, and fading from its walls—
How often from its hingeless door
I have watched—dead leaf, like the ghost of a mouse,
Rasping the worn brick floor—
The snows of the weir descending below,
And their thunderous waterfall.

Fall—fall: dark, garrulous rumour,
Until I could listen no more.
Could listen no more—for beauty with sorrow
Is a burden hard to be borne;
The evening light on the foam, and the swans, there;
That music, remote, forlorn.

WALTER DE LA MARE

The Comb

My mother sate me at her glass;
This necklet of bright flowers she wove;
Crisscross her gentle hands did pass,
And wound in my hair her love.

Deep in the mirror our glances met,
And grieved, lest from her care I roam,
She kissed me through her tears, and set
On high this spangling comb.

WALTER DE LA MARE

The Departure of the Good Dæmon

What can I do in Poetry,
Now the good Spirit's gone from me?
Why nothing now, but lonely sit,
And over-read what I have writ.

ROBERT HERRICK

Crossing the Bar

Sunset and evening star,
   And one clear call for me!
And may there be no moaning of the bar,
   When I put out to sea,

But such a tide as moving seems asleep,
   Too full for sound and foam
When that which drew from out the boundless deep
   Turns again home.

Twilight and evening bell,
   And after that the dark!
And may there be no sadness of farewell,
   When I embark;

For tho' from out our bourne of Time and Place
   The flood may bear me far,
I hope to see my Pilot face to face
   When I have crost the bar.

ALFRED TENNYSON

Crossing Alone the Nighted Ferry

Crossing alone the nighted ferry
   With the one coin for fee,
Whom, on the wharf of Lethe waiting,
   Count you to find? Not me.

[216]

The brisk fond lackey to fetch and carry,
    The true, sick-hearted slave,
Expect him not in the just city
    And free land of the grave.

A. E. HOUSMAN

To a Poet a Thousand Years Hence

I who am dead a thousand years,
    And wrote this sweet archaic song,
Send you my words for messengers
    The way I shall not pass along.

I care not if you bridge the seas,
    Or ride secure the cruel sky,
Or build consummate palaces
    Of metal or of masonry.

But have you wine and music still,
    And statues and a bright-eyed love,
And foolish thoughts of good and ill,
    And prayers to them who sit above?

How shall we conquer? Like a wind
    That falls at eve our fancies blow,
And old Mæonides the blind
    Said it three thousand years ago.

O friend unseen, unborn, unknown,
    Student of our sweet English tongue,
Read out my words at night, alone:
    I was a poet, I was young.

Since I can never see your face,
    And never shake you by the hand,
I send my soul through time and space
    To greet you. You will understand.

JAMES ELROY FLECKER

A Letter from a Girl to Her Own Old Age

Listen, and when thy hand this paper presses,
O time-worn woman, think of her who blesses
What thy thin fingers touch, with her caresses.

O mother, for the weight of years that break thee!
O daughter, for slow Time must yet awake thee,
And from the changes of my heart must make thee.

O fainting traveller, morn is grey in heaven.
Dost thou remember how the clouds were driven?
And are they calm about the fall of even?

Pause near the ending of thy long migration,
For this one sudden hour of desolation
Appeals to one hour of thy meditation.

Suffer, O silent one, that I remind thee
Of the great hills that stormed the sky behind thee,
Of the wild winds of power that have resigned thee.

Know that the mournful plain where thou must wander
Is but a grey and silent world, but ponder
The misty mountains of the morning yonder.

Listen:—the mountain winds with rain were fretting,
And sudden gleams the mountain-tops besetting.
I cannot let thee fade to death, forgetting.

What part of this wild heart of mine I know not
Will follow with thee where the great winds blow not,
And where the young flowers of the mountain grow not.

I have not writ this letter of divining
To make a glory of thy silent pining,
A triumph of thy mute and strange declining.

Only one youth, and the bright life is shrouded.
Only one morning, and the day was clouded.
And one old age with all regrets is crowded.

O hush, O hush! Thy tears my words are steeping.
O hush, hush, hush! So full, the fount of weeping?
Poor eyes, so quickly moved, so near to sleeping?

Pardon the girl; such strange desires beset her.
Poor woman, lay aside the mournful letter
That breaks thy heart; the one who wrote, forget her:

The one who now thy faded features guesses,
With filial fingers thy grey hair caresses,
With morning tears thy mournful twilight blesses.

ALICE MEYNELL

An End

Love, strong as Death, is dead.
Come, let us make his bed
Among the dying flowers:
A green turf at his head;
And a stone at his feet,
Whereon we may sit
In the quiet evening hours.

He was born in the Spring,
And died before the harvesting:
On the last warm Summer day
He left us; he would not stay
For Autumn twilight cold and gray.
Sit we by his grave, and sing
He is gone away.

To few chords and sad and low
Sing we so:
Be our eyes fixed on the grass
Shadow-veiled as the years pass,
While we think of all that was
In the long ago.

CHRISTINA ROSSETTI

Upon His Departure Hence

Thus I
Pass by,
And die:
As one,
Unknown,
And gone:
I'm made
A shade,
And laid
I' the grave
There have
My cave.
Where tell
I dwell,
Farewell.

ROBERT HERRICK

Of the Last Verses in the Book
Poems, 1686

When we for Age could neither read nor write
The subject made us able to indite.
The Soul with nobler Resolutions deckt,
The Body stooping, does Herself erect:
No Mortal Parts are requisite to raise
Her, that Unbody'd can her Maker praise.

The Seas are quiet, when the Winds give o'er
So calm are we, when Passions are no more:
For then we know how vain it was to boast
Of fleeting Things, so certain to be lost.
Clouds of Affection from our younger Eyes
Conceal that emptiness, which Age descries.

The Soul's dark Cottage, batter'd and decay'd,
Lets in new Light thro' chinks that time has made.
Stronger by weakness, wiser Men become
As they draw near to their Eternal home:
Leaving the old, both Worlds at once they view,
That stand upon the threshold of the New.

EDMUND WALLER

O Sweetheart, Hear Thou

O Sweetheart, hear thou
  Your lover's tale;
A man shall have sorrow
  When friends him fail.

For he shall know then
  Friends be untrue
And a little ashes
  Their words come to.

But one unto him
  Will softly move
And softly woo him
  In ways of love.

His hand is under
  Her smooth round breast;
So he who has sorrow
  Shall have rest.

JAMES JOYCE

Index of poets and works

[225]

[229]

[231]

Index of first lines

[235]